Protect You

Instalove Age-Gap Romance

Nichole Rose

Contents

Dedication

In Loving Memory of C. Hawkins.

August 10, 1982 – December 12, 2020
Thank you for the laughter and sunshine you brought into my life. You'll always be a BB.

About the Book

THIS SEAL WILL WAGE war to win a future with this feisty girl.

Bryant

I loved Gia Duncan the day I met her.

But I knew I had to ship out, so I said nothing.

I'm back now, and all I want is to claim my girl.

I think I have a real chance until I say something stupid.

Now she wants nothing to do with me, but that's too bad.

An angry client is targeting her, and I'm her first line of defense.

I just left a war zone.

I'll wage another if that's what it takes to win her heart and her safety.

She's mine to protect, and I'm taking no prisoners.

Gia

I thought Bryant Denver cared about me.

But I wrote him every week. He never wrote back.

Now he's accused me of sleeping with my brother.

And saved me from a crazy client.

He says I'm his and swears he's not going anywhere.

I'm so afraid to let him in again.

He broke my heart once.

Can I trust him to protect it this time?

Warning

This older SEAL isn't afraid to fight dirty to claim his curvy younger woman. If office romance, over-the-top men on a mission, and feisty heroines make you happy, you'll love Gia and Bryant. This sweet, steamy romance from Nichole Rose comes complete with a sticky-sweet and guaranteed HEA.

Chapter One
Bryant

"STOP STALLING AND GET out of the truck," I mutter to myself for the fourth time in as many minutes, staring out the windshield at the small Craftsman bungalow ahead. It's well-kept, with bright curtains over the windows and potted plants lining the small porch. The yard needs to be mowed, which makes me smile.

Gia Duncan hates yard work and isn't afraid to let you know it. The girl has more houseplants than most people have underwear but put a mower in front of her and she's more likely to set it on fire than use it. Before I deployed, I mowed for her. I guess she hasn't found anyone to replace me since I've been gone.

God, I hope she hasn't found anyone to replace me, in more ways than one.

I'm so fucking in love with Gia it's almost laughable. And she doesn't have a clue. I've been gone for almost thirteen months...the longest of my life. Being away from her was pure hell. I loathed every fucking minute of it. I spent my days battling terrorists and rescuing civilians, and my nights driving myself crazy, thinking about Gia, wondering if she missed me as much as I missed her. If she was happy. If she was taking care of herself instead of taking care of everyone else like she always does.

Her weekly letters were the only bright spot during my time in Syria, the hope I clung to that she might feel the same way about me. That I might actually have a chance of making her mine. They were full of laughter and office gossip, of those little pieces of her that I find so fucking cute. Like her obsession with reality television, and the steamy books she reads only on her Kindle because she thinks no one can tell she's reading erotica. She's wrong about that. Her face gives her away every time.

Her letters kept me going when nothing else did.

Until she stopped writing two months ago.

I can't even blame her for it. I'm the one who left without telling her how I feel about her. I'm the one who didn't have the balls to send the one letter I wrote her, the one where I poured my fucking heart out, told her that I've been in love with her since the day she started at Davis Financial Group.

We spent six months getting to know each other, laughing together, hanging out. She gave me shit about watching football. I gave her shit about the Kardashians. I brought her coffee every morning. She brought me leftovers. We spent our lunchbreaks in my office, every day for six months. She rambled about everything. I smiled like a crazy person.

Leaving without telling her how I feel was bullshit but I didn't want to put that on either of us. The shit I had to deal with over there was hard enough without having to think about my girl being here alone, heartbroken because I wasn't with her.

Had I told her, I'm not so sure I would have been able to leave her. As soon as I held her in my arms for the first time, it would have been over with. I would have found a way to stay...leaving my team without the best sniper they had. That wasn't an option. Their lives—and countless others—depended on me, and I was committed.

When all you have in the world is your word, you learn quick just how much value it holds. Besides, walking away from the armed forces without totally fucking yourself isn't exactly an easy thing to do.

But Gia? There's nothing I wouldn't sacrifice to be the reason she smiles in the morning, or the reason that adorable blush stains her cheeks when she reads her dirty books. I'd walk through hell for that girl, fight a thousand wars.

"So get your ass out of the car and go claim her," I mutter to myself.

Right.

Step one: stop being a little bitch.

I take a deep breath and pop the door to my truck, hoping like hell she's actually home and her car is just in the garage. I slam the door closed and then stride up the driveway. It's cracked in places, the cement buckling where tree roots and weeds search for sunlight. I can't remember the last time my hands shook like this. Never once when my finger was on the trigger, that's for damn sure.

I've always been cool under pressure, able to handle whatever is thrown at me. This is different. *Gia* is different, in a million different ways and for a million different reasons. She's absolutely fucking stunning, for one. With glossy auburn hair, creamy ivory skin, and bright hazel eyes rimmed in green, I can't take my eyes off her when she's nearby. I've never seen eyes like hers before.

All it takes is one look in those pretty pools to realize she's not only beautiful, but she's also intelligent as hell. Ivy League educated, graduated early at the top of her class, literal member of Mensa intelligent. The girl knows exactly what she's talking about, regardless of what she's talking about. Her clients tend to underestimate her because she's young, female, and gorgeous. Watching her destroy their misogynistic assumptions is a hell of a turn on.

She's curvy, maybe five foot eight, with the longest, sexiest legs. Trying to keep myself from wrapping them around my waist and plowing into her until she's screaming is a never-ending struggle when I'm near her. I want to make love to her so fucking badly it's torture. I've fantasized about it daily for a year and a half. My cock is raw, but the fucker keeps hoisting the sail. Every single time I think about Gia.

At twenty-five, she's a full decade younger than I am. Ask me if it matters.

She's sarcastic and funny as hell, but she never jokes at the expense of anyone except herself. People love her because she loves people. She's nurturing, always trying to look out and take care of everyone else. She's not content unless everyone in her little world is happy and thriving. God knows, she teased the shit out of me until I was laughing on more than one occasion.

I've been in the military my entire adult life. The things I've seen and done are the things that make you lose sleep at night. The kind of things that stay with you. They haunt better men than me, get the best of them sometimes, too.

Gia, though? Gia always seemed to know where my head was at or when things were bad. She always found a way to make even the worst of it lighter. When I was with her, all the nightmares, all the demons, all the bullshit just...fell away. The only thing that existed was her. I was at peace when she was nearby. Happy. Probably for the first time in my life.

When she has kids—and she wants a lot of them—she's going to be an incredible mom.

I plan to be the man who gives her all those babies.

I inhale another deep breath and then rap on the door, two quick knocks followed by a slower third one, so she knows it's me. She doesn't have a peephole. I tried to convince her to let me put one in because she's forever flinging the door wide open without knowing who is on the other side of it. She told me absolutely not. Her landlord wouldn't allow it.

If I have my way, he won't be an issue much longer because she'll be living with me.

Shit. Maybe I should have brought her flowers or something?

Footsteps sound through the house and then the chain scrapes on the other side of the door. I shove my hands into my pockets to hide how fucking nervous I am about seeing her again. My right one lands on the letter I've been carrying around for a year...the one I never sent her.

Don't know why I carry it with me, but it's been in my pocket every day for the last thirteen months. Her address on the envelope is smudged and wearing off in places because I touch it so often. Every time I pulled it out of my pocket while deployed, I intended to send it to her, but I never did.

The door flies open.

"What the fuck?" I growl, staring in shock at the man standing on the other side. He's definitely not fucking Gia. Matter of fact, I don't know who the hell he is, but he looks awful fucking comfortable without a shirt or shoes, his jeans slung low on his hips. He's maybe six-one, with a dark, crewcut hair and blue eyes. He's big, but he seems young.

Then again, Gia's young too.

Is she *dating* this motherfucker?

Oh, hell no.

"Can I help you?" he asks, looking confused to see me standing there. That makes two of us because he's definitely not who I expected.

"Yeah. Who the fuck are you?" I growl.

"Uh, did you forget the pizza?" he asks, which doesn't answer my question.

"What?"

"You're supposed to be delivering a pizza," he says, talking slow, like he thinks I don't understand what he's saying. "Pepperoni, extra cheese, extra sauce, sourdough?"

Gia's favorite. She loves ordering takeout from Noni's. Not because she's a big pizza fan, but because she adores Noni. I think she'd singlehandedly keep the place afloat if she could afford to do it. Luckily, business is thriving, and Noni's doesn't need saving.

"Do you have the pizza or not?" the guy asks, clearly losing patience with me.

"I'm not your fucking delivery driver," I snap. "Where's Gia?"

"Who's asking?"

I open my mouth tell him I'm her man and then snap it closed. Judging by the claws currently working on my insides and the evidence standing in front of me, I'm not her man. I'm just the asshole who waited too late to tell her how he felt.

Fuck me.

Is *he* the reason she stopped writing me?

"Name's Bryant," I mutter.

"She's still at work. Can I help you with something.?" he says again, eyeing me like he thinks I'm trying to get inside to steal her valuables or something. He looks like he'd be more comfortable playing that role than I would, though.

When I don't answer, he waves his hand in front of my face as if trying to get my attention.

"How do you know Gia? Are you on something? You're acting shady as shit right now," he says, narrowing his eyes at me. Suspicion glints in the blue depths.

"Why? You interested in buying?" I snap. Gia would never get involved with someone on drugs, so I know this kid is clean, but I say it anyway, just to piss him off.

It works.

His jaw hardens, his glare turning glacial. "I think you need to get the fuck off my porch now."

"You're right about that," I mutter, and then I stare at him for another second before turning to jog down the steps, headed back to my truck. The door slams behind me.

My heart pounds, my blood pressure rising. I can't believe she's with this jackass. Guess that's what I get for not telling her how I felt, for not asking her to wait for me.

Shit. Why didn't I ask her to wait for me?

Oh, right. Because I'm a fucking idiot.

I climb into my truck, slam the door, and then just sit there for a minute, trying to convince myself to let her go and move on. That I don't need to go to Davis Financial to see her. Seeing her when I know she's with someone else isn't going to help me move on.

I should listen to the little voice shouting all this shit at me.

But I don't. Of-fucking-course I don't.

I crank the engine, back out, and head west.

Traffic is light, which is surprising until I realize it's already after six. Gia works a lot of late hours and early mornings. She pushes herself harder than anyone I know. Before I deployed, I made sure to stick around and send her home at a decent hour. She hated when I told her what to do and would give me the cutest fucking scowl, but she always went.

When I found out she was going in early, I started making sure I was there early too, just to see her and that smile. God, I miss that fucking smile. I don't know if she's serious about her boy toy back there...and I don't know if I'm willing to let her go, either. She was made for me. I was damn sure made for her because no one else has ever made me feel like she does.

Unlike a lot of the men on my team, sleeping around never interested me much. I can't remember the last time I went on a date with anyone, let alone the last time I slept with anyone. Getting involved when I could be deployed at any moment never appealed to me before Gia. But this last deployment was my final tour. I'm out now.

The future I envisioned for myself, the one where Gia's mine, feels like it's slowly slipping through my fingers.

It takes ten minutes to get to Davis Financial. The building is locked up, but that's not a big deal. I still have my keycards. Grant hoped I'd come back to work for him once I finished my final tour. But I don't know if there's still a place for me here. A lot can change in a year.

I pull into the parking garage and spot Gia's blue Prius parked in her usual spot. It's too fucking far from the elevator. I must have told her a thousand times to move her car closer if she was going to work late, but she never listened. She always laughed and told me I was just being paranoid, that she was perfectly safe with me there. Which was true, but still. What if I hadn't been there? The parking garage might be secure during daylight hours, but people get up to all sorts of shady shit when the lights go out. She teased me when I told her that.

It made me crazy in the best way possible.

I pull in beside her car and hop out. I don't have a plan. Don't know what I'm going to say to her. I tell myself I just want to see her again and make sure she's okay before I move on. But I'm honest enough to admit when I'm deluding myself. There is no moving on from a girl like Gia Duncan. Not for me. Not ever.

There's a Bentley pulled up sideways in the three spots closest to the elevator, the driver still behind the wheel. He lifts his hand in greeting but doesn't let down the window. I'm guessing his boss is the reason Gia's here so late. Millionaires and billionaires don't keep normal hours. In my experience, most of them don't give a shit if they inconvenience anyone else, especially not when it comes to their money. Quite frankly, they can be pricks.

I don't know how Gia deals with their shit all day, every day. With her brain, she could go anywhere, do anything, but she's wanted to work in finance ever since she watched *Working Girl* with her mom when she was a little girl. She loves what she does and the people she works with. Even if some of the clients are uptight assholes, Grant watches out for his people. He has no qualms about firing a client if they cross a line. He's an all-around good guy, one of the handful of billionaires I've met who aren't self-absorbed dicks. He's one of my closest friends.

I bypass the elevator and take the stairs. The jog up to the third floor does nothing to calm me down. As soon as I shove the stairwell access door open, I hear a man's raised voice coming from down the hallway.

"You stupid bitch!" he shouts. "You lost a million fucking dollars!"

"No, sir, I did not," Gia says. She sounds calm, but I hear the little tremor in her voice.

He probably doesn't, but I do. I know this girl. I know everything about her. I know when she's tired and when she's flustered. When she's happy and when she's sad. Right now, she's scared.

One thing my girl shouldn't ever be is afraid.

No one talks to Gia like this motherfucker is, not if they want to keep breathing. I've fought and killed for this country. I'll do it for her too, without hesitation.

I stomp down the hall, fury and adrenaline pumping through me with every beat of my heart.

"Do you even understand how much money I lost because of you?" he shouts, his voice turning shrill at the end.

"I warned you repeatedly that you were getting involved with a pyramid scheme, Mr. Laughlin," Gia says, still speaking calmly. "I firmly advised you against investing in the company. You ignored my advice and demanded I sink a million dollars into it. You signed a liability waiver, which detailed my concerns. I'm sorry it didn't work out, but the blame rests with you, not me. If you'd like to talk to Mr. Davis about it, you're welcome to do so, but I think you need to leave now."

"I'm not going anywhere until I get my money!" he roars. "You owe me a million dollars."

"Mr. Laughlin, I said leave," she says. "You aren't thinking clearly and are being incredibly rude. I may manage your account, but that doesn't give you the right to talk to me the way you have been tonight."

"You work for me."

"Not anymore!" she snaps, losing her patience with him. "I'm terminating our business relationship, effective immediately. Mr. Davis can find another advisor to work with you if he'd like."

"You think you can get rid of me that easily?" he roars. "Either show me the waiver or give me the money."

Something crashes against the wall and shatters.

I'm running before Gia has a chance to cry out in fear.

I round the corner, enraged. My rage grows when I see the scene unfolding in her office. She's backed into the corner behind her desk, with Laughlin towering over her, screaming in her face. As far as I can tell, he's maybe forty-five. He's not much taller than she is, but he's three times her size, beefy with ruddy skin and thin hair. A broken picture frame is on the floor nearby, far enough away so I know it didn't hit her.

That's the only thing that saves his miserable life.

I grab the collar of his thousand-dollar suit and fling him away from her. He lands against her desk, damn near knocking it over. Shit falls off the other side, crashing to the floor in a mess of paperwork and knickknacks.

"Stay away from her," I growl, getting in his face.

"Who do you–?"

"Think I am?" I finish before he can, my hands clenched into tight fists to keep me from wrapping them around the excess skin of his throat. "Your worst goddamn nightmare, Laughlin. If you want to keep breathing, I suggest you take her advice and get the hell out of here."

"She owes me a million dollars," he says, spittle flying from his lips. He's like a rabid dog, enraged and foaming at the mouth. Malice glitters in his bloodshot eyes.

"She doesn't owe you shit. Don't even look at her," I warn him when his brown eyes flit from me to Gia. "You're lucky I'm letting you walk out of here after you assaulted and disrespected her. I've killed better men than you for less. If I were you, I'd go before I change my mind."

He blanches, his face turning white and then red with rage. A vein in his temple bulges. He opens his mouth, only to snap it closed again when I growl a wordless warning. He jerks on the bottom of his jacket, righting it. One beefy hand runs through his thinning hair, smoothing the wispy black strands.

"Go," I growl. "Now."

He sniffs loudly and smooths his hair again.

"This isn't over," he snaps at Gia before storming toward the door. It slams behind him so hard the frame cracks.

"Jerk," Gia mutters from behind me.

I stay where I'm at for a moment instead of turning to look at her, not trusting that I'll be able to keep my hands off her if I see her right now. My heart still pounds, sending my protective instincts soaring as adrenaline rushes through me in a tidal wave. If she's still afraid, I won't be able to keep myself from scooping her up into my arms to hold her...or from going after the son of a bitch I just kicked out of here.

Treating women with disrespect pisses me off on a good day. Today isn't one of those...and Gia isn't just any woman. She might not know it yet—Boy Toy might not either—but she's mine. And no one makes my woman feel unsafe in her own office. Fuck that noise.

"You okay, Gia baby?" I ask, sucking air into my lungs in deep inhales.

"I think I peed a little," she whispers.

Jesus Christ. I missed her.

"Did he hurt you, sweetheart?"

"No. He didn't touch me. He broke my picture frame though, and I liked that one!"

A groan rips from deep within my chest at the sound of her offended outrage. How she manages to make me want to laugh when I'm pissed, I don't know. But I have to fight to keep the smile off my face.

"Are you really here, Bryant?" she whispers a moment later, a tremor in her voice.

I spin to face her, unable to stop myself.

"Jesus," I breathe, stumbling slightly.

Even though she's pale and shaking, seeing her again almost drops me to the floor. She's gotten more beautiful in the last year. Her hair is longer, hanging halfway down her back. Those multi-colored eyes are wide and watery, but still the prettiest mix of hazel and emerald green I've ever seen.

Her black dress has a piece that makes it look like a blazer, with two buttons under her right breast. It hugs her curves just right, giving her an hourglass shape. The dress ends just above the knees, but she's indecently sexy in the damn thing. She could be in a burlap sack, and I'd think the same thing. She's too goddamn perfect to be real.

She stares at me for a long, silent moment as if processing that I'm really standing in front of her. Her gaze races up and down my body, examining me from head to toe. My hair is shorter than it was when I left and I've gained muscle mass, but I know that's not what she's searching for. She wants to know that I made it home safely.

"I'm all right, Gia baby," I rasp.

My voice seems to snap her back to reality.

"I missed you so much!" she cries, rushing across the room toward me.

Right before she flings herself at me, I take a step back, my hands lifted. I can't feel her in my arms and then let her go. If she touches me, I'm going to kiss her. I won't do that until she's done with him. Regardless of how much I loathe her little boy toy, I won't turn her into a cheater. She'd regret it for the rest of her life.

She stumbles to a stop, her beautiful face plummeting from joy to sorrow in a single heartbeat. Her eyes scan my face, a question in them. "Bryant?" she says, her voice hesitant, more vulnerable than it was with that dick screaming at her.

I want to hold her so fucking badly it hurts. My knees threaten to buckle under the strain of keeping my distance. I shove my hands into my pockets, lock my legs, and shift my gaze from hers.

Silence grows between us, so loud it's deafening. That's never been us, never been our way. Gia chatters nonstop, sharing every thought in her head, peppering you with a million questions. I love that about her, how open and honest she is, and how eager she is to know every single thing she can about everyone she meets. She soaks it up like a sponge. Doesn't matter what you tell her, she never, ever forgets it.

"I wrote you," she whispers into the silence. "D-did you get my letters?"

"I did," I mutter, guilt pinging through me. I want to tell her that I read them so often I memorized every word. And then I get a mental image of her boy toy and possessive jealousy seethes through me. I chance another look at her. "Does your boyfriend know you were writing me?"

She blinks at me, confusion in her gaze. "What?"

"Your boyfriend," I growl, emphasizing the word *boy*. "The jackass living with you?"

"What are you talking about?" she asks, looking at me like I'm crazy. "I don't live with anyone, Bryant."

"No?" I quirk a brow. "He seemed awful fucking cozy when I was there half an hour ago. Answered the door half naked."

"You went to my house?" she asks, gaping at me.

"Don't think he'd like knowing you were writing another man while sleeping with him, Gia," I say instead of answering her question. Of course I went to see her. Where the hell else would I go?

She stares at me for another long moment. I can see the storm brewing in her eyes. Green bleeds into the hazel, lending her eyes an almost preternatural brightness. They're stunning. *She* is stunning.

"Wait a minute," she says, her voice dropping to a sultry growl. My girl may be sweet as pie, but she's equally as feisty. She doesn't take shit from anyone, least of all me. Her eyes narrow on me, her cheeks flushing. "You went by my house and someone answered the door, so you just assumed I'm *sleeping* with him? That he has permission to tell me who I can and can't write?"

"Something like that," I mutter.

Which is clearly the wrong thing, judging by the way her expression darkens. I almost expect to see her head spin as she splutters in rage. Her mouth opens and then closes several times, her entire body going taut.

"Are you kidding me right now? I wrote you every week for a freaking year, Bryant, and you never once wrote me back! Now you come in here, pissed off and making assumptions, treating me like I'm a-a cheater because I thought you were my friend? You don't have that right."

I want to tell her that she's wrong...but I can't because she isn't. I don't have that right yet. I want to ask if I was only ever a friend to her, but I don't do that either. If she says yes, the answer might break me in ways war never could.

"You're right," I say, my jaw clenching so hard my back teeth ache in protest. "I don't."

I don't think she expected me to agree. It deflates her a bit.

"You going to be good here?"

"I'm fine."

"I'll wait for you to finish up and walk you to your car."

"You don't have to do that. I said I'm fine," she mutters, scowling daggers at me.

"Going to anyway."

"Dammit, Bryant," she sighs. Her head droops forward, the rest of the fire going out of her. She curls in on herself and stands there for a long moment, looking small and vulnerable.

I've never seen her look this way before. My heart breaks for the second time today, and yet again, I only have myself to blame. I want to pull her into my arms and tell her how I feel about her, tell her I'm sorry...tell her everything. But I don't.

I'm an idiot. What can I say?

"I'll wait in the hall while you gather your shit," I say and then duck out of her office before I say anything else and hurt her even more. As soon as I step into the hall, I feel like an ass. No. I *know* I'm an ass. She didn't deserve to be treated that way, especially when I never told her how I felt. I just expected her to wait.

Why would a girl like Gia wait for a guy like me? God knows, she can do better. I'm a former SEAL with a high school diploma, no family, and no job at the moment...not exactly a great catch for a woman like her. Doesn't mean I have to like it though.

She stomps around her office, slamming shit around, which makes me smile. She's so fucking cute when she's mad. It doesn't happen often, but when it does, she hisses and spits like a little kitten. I must have fantasized a thousand times about pissing her off and then putting my mouth all over her until she was purring again.

I can hear her mumbling under her breath but can't tell what she's saying. Doubt any of it is complimentary. She curses like a sailor when she's pissed. It sounds completely ridiculous in that sweet voice, but I love it.

Who am I kidding?

I love everything about this girl. I'm so fucking gone over her that it's tearing me up inside.

"Let's go," she says a moment later, stomping out into the hall with her bag slung over her shoulder. She shoots a death glare at me and then sniffs and turns her face away, already hurrying toward the elevator.

I push away from the wall and fall into step behind her. When I see the way her perfect ass fills out that dress, I bite my tongue so hard I taste blood. She stabs the elevator button like she wishes it were my face.

The wait for the damn thing seems to drag on forever. I don't miss her relieved exhale when it finally arrives. We ride down in complete silence. We've been on this elevator together a thousand times. When I was overseas, I thought of a thousand different things I'd do to her in here the next time I got her alone with no one around and no cameras to catch us. Now we're here...and I'm not allowed to touch her.

I curse under my breath.

She jerks like I startled her and then takes a step away from me.

I open my mouth to apologize for being an ass, but the elevator shudders to a stop. Before I can say anything, the doors slide open and she storms out like she's going into battle. I hurry to follow her in case Laughlin is still lurking around, but his car is gone.

"I've got it from here," she says over her shoulder...like that's going to keep me from following behind her like a lost dog.

"I'll walk you," I say, not willing to take any chances with her.

She huffs loudly.

I bite my lip to keep from laughing. She's so damn cute. Jesus. She's gotten even cuter since I left. The way her ass sways in her skirt has my mouth watering. Reconciling the fact that I can't touch her with the fact that, in my mind, she's always been mine, is fucking me up. I want to grip that ass while she's riding me so goddamn badly, it's killing me.

When we get to her car, she pops the locks and tosses her bag inside before turning back to face me. She opens her mouth like she's going to say something, and then shakes her head as if to rid herself of the urge. She climbs inside her car without a word.

"Guess I'll see you around, Gia baby," I say, my heart fucking bleeding.

"Yeah. See you around."

I take a step backward, toward my truck.

"Hey, Bryant?"

"Yeah?"

"The guy at my house is my little brother, you big jerk," she says and then slams the car door in my face.

Wait. What?

That was her little brother, Dante?

Jesus Christ.

Her car hums to life as I stand there, slack-jawed, trying to process exactly how badly I've fucked up. Judging by the way she peels out of the parking garage like she's trying to qualify in the Indy 500...it's a lot.

"Fuuuuck," I groan as her taillights disappear.

If ever I needed proof that I am, in fact, a big jerk, I now have it.

Chapter Two

Gia

"I HATE MEN," I growl, staring around my office. It looks like a hurricane swept through. My favorite picture frame is shattered on the floor. Half of the stuff on my desk is in a pile in front of it. My lamp is knocked askew, and I think one of the wheels on my chair is broken.

All because Joe Laughlin thinks taking advice from a woman is the equivalent of taking advice from an airhead. If he would have listened one of the fifteen times that I told him that his buddy was running a pyramid scheme, he wouldn't be out a million dollars. But no.

I make a mental note to add smashing the patriarchy to my list of things to do today, and then set about putting my office back in order before Grant sees it and flips out. Not because it's a mess. If he cared about messes, my work bestie, Holly Sterling, would have been fired ages ago. But because he does not take kindly to clients who don't treat us well.

I'd rather break the news to him gently.

"Hey," Holly says, popping her head into my office.

"Hey. You're back." I look up at her from where I'm crouched on the floor, picking up the last few things that were knocked off my desk last night. Her red hair hangs in ringlets around her face. Her cheeks are pink and her green eyes sparkle. She's always been so adorable, but she looks so happy since she and Ian Sterling got married last year.

She just gave birth to their baby boy last month and is supposed to be on maternity leave. She's so in love with their baby. So is Ian for that matter. Even though Holly should be resting, she still runs circles around him, which he loves. The way he looks at her makes me so happy for her. For a long time, she was scared to even meet him. But he took one look at her and fell head over heels.

Everyone here is falling in love. It's like Woodstock around here most of the time, except without the drugs. We're all crazy enough without those.

"Only to see you," she says. "I heard Bryant's back."

Jeez. News travels fast around this place.

A pang shoots through me at the sound of his name.

"I saw him last night," I say, dropping a trampled envelope in the trash as I rise to my feet.

"Shut the front door!" Holly gasps, her red lips popping open. "You saw him last night?"

"Yep." I set a file on my desk and cross my arms over my chest like that's going to stop my heart from breaking again. Bryant Denver is, without a doubt, a big jerk.

I'm so angry with him.

I'm also so in love with him it's pathetic. Which is a bit of a problem considering that I've sworn off men forever because of him. Who knew that you really could want to kiss someone and strangle them at the same exact time?

We were close before he deployed. We spent all of our free time together. I thought he felt the same way I did. I waited and waited and waited for him to make a move, but he never did. I figured maybe it was because he knew he was being deployed and didn't want to ask me to wait. He's that type of guy...at least I always thought he was.

Until last night. The Bryant I met last night is not the Bryant I knew.

I can't stand it. I miss my Bryant like crazy.

He is one of the most beautiful men I've ever met. He's maybe six-two, with incredible green eyes and a smirk I want to kiss off his handsome face. He keeps his dark hair short, I guess because he's been in the military for so long, but he has a little cowlick. Every time he's close, my hands actually itch with the desire to reach out and smooth it.

He's built like a brick wall. He's even more muscular now than he was then. Before he was deployed, he worked as the head of security here. There's not a lot to do around here, so he mostly spent his days giving all the women here something pretty to look at. But on the few occasion we did have someone like Laughlin get out of hand, he tossed them out without even breaking a sweat.

I'm a virgin, but I've probably thought a million times about what it would be like to be with him. Would he be sweet and tender? Or would he be rough and demanding? Or both? I've wanted to find out since the day we met.

When he never wrote me back, I thought maybe he wasn't getting my letters since they were being routed through another base. Or maybe that he just didn't want to tell me about his time over there. Before he left, he was always so tightlipped about his time in warzones. He used to tell me that the darkness he dealt with didn't belong in my life. He was always protective of me...overly so, sometimes.

I didn't mind though. It made me happy that he cared enough to want to look out for me. I almost admitted how I felt about him a thousand times, but I was so afraid I'd ruin our friendship if I did. Having even a piece of him was better than not having him at all.

I worried about him endlessly when he was gone. Every day, I scoured the news to make sure he was safe. I read every article about the troops in Syria that I could get my hands on. I'm one of the only people who knew that's where he was really going. Everyone thinks he was in Iraq, but he told me the truth, even though doing so could have gotten him into trouble. I've kept that secret for him for all this time.

It was almost pathetic how much time I spent searching out even the tiniest hint of him, just to be close to him. Just to know he was safe. I worried about him every damn day...but he couldn't even pick up a pen to tell me he was alive.

Finding that out last night broke my heart into tiny pieces. I wanted there to be an explanation so badly, and there isn't. I'm angrier about that than I am about the fact that he accused me of sleeping with my little brother.

"Tell me everything!" Holly demands, practically levitating into my office and then dropping down into a chair. Unlike her office, you can actually sit down in mine. She and I are complete opposites, yet we get along so well. I love her to death. She's completely crazy, of course. But it's one of the things I love most about her.

She glances around, her expression morphing from excited to confused as she documents the state of my desk and the shattered picture frame. "Did you two have dirty hot sex in here?"

"No," I snort, shaking my head.

"Oh. What...never mind. We'll come back to this"—she points a finger at the mess and twirls it around to indicate what she means—"in a minute. Tell me about Bryant."

"I guess he stopped by the house to see me," I explain, giving her the CliffsNotes version. "Dante answered the door since he's been here visiting Vanderbilt this week. Bryant got the wrong impression and thought we were dating. Right?" I say when Holly makes a face at the thought of me and my brother dating. "He came here afterward. One of my clients was acting like an asshole. Bryant kicked him out of here and then demanded to know if Dante knew I was writing another man while sleeping with him."

"He did not," Holly says, her eyes going comically wide.

"He did." I scowl at the reminder.

"So he did get your letters."

"Yeah, he got them."

Holly's eyes narrow. She's the only person on the planet who knows how I feel about Bryant, or that I wrote him every week. I guess that's a good thing. Now the rest of the world won't have to know that I can't take a hint.

"We argued about it. He walked me out to my car, and that was that," I sigh. "I told him Dante was my brother before I drove off."

"Whoa," Holly says. "That's a lot."

"Yeah." I take a deep breath and then exhale, refusing to cry over Bryant again. I was one of the only girls in the gifted and talented program throughout my school years. Some of the guys were cool about it. Some weren't. Little boys can be ruthless when they feel threatened by a girl. My mom always told me to cry as much as I needed to cry...but once I was done, not to do it for the same boy again. This situation is different, but I figure the advice probably still applies. I cried over him last night. I won't cry over him again today. Nope. No way.

"What are you going to do?" Holly asks.

"What can I do?" I say with a shrug. "I waited for him for a year. He's back, and now I know he doesn't feel the same way. He didn't even try to call me last night after I told him that Dante is my brother."

"Gia," Holly whispers, her face falling.

"No," I say, hating that she's upset on my behalf. She doesn't need to be upset for me, especially not when she just had a baby. "It's fine. It's whatever. I wanted to know how he felt, and now I know."

I wish my stupid heart would take the hint.

"He came to see you," she reminds me. "Doesn't that mean anything?"

"I don't know. All this time, he's been getting my letters and never wrote back. He may have come to see me last night, but he let me worry about him for an entire year. And then he made me feel like I did something wrong by caring enough to write him. I don't think a man who cares would do that, do you?"

"I...don't know," Holly says, clearly hesitant. "Maybe he had a reason for not writing back."

"He made me feel so dirty," I whisper.

"Good dirty or bad dirty?" Holly asks, wiggling her eyebrows.

I narrow my eyes on her.

"Sorry, sorry," she says, putting her hands up. "I couldn't resist. But seriously...maybe he came to see you last night because he does care, but then he saw Dante and thought the worst. Obviously, he didn't handle it well, but I don't think he would have even said anything about it if he weren't jealous."

"Maybe," I mutter doubtfully, squashing the little seed of hope threatening to bloom. Even if he was jealous, it doesn't change the fact that he ignored my existence for an entire freaking year.

"You know what this means," Holly says.

"What?" I ask, not liking her tone.

"We have to get drunk," she whispers as if she's telling me a big secret.

I stare at her for just a second and then laugh. "Holly, you're breastfeeding. You can't drink."

"I wouldn't give the baby drunk milk," she says, rolling her eyes at me. And then she pats her boobs. "These things make more than enough. My freezer is stocked up."

"You're crazy, you know that?" I say, shaking my head.

"I know." She grins.

"Ian's never going to let you get drunk with me."

"He will."

"He won't."

"Yes, he will," she says. "He lets me do whatever I want."

"Uh-huh," I say, laughing. "Go ahead and call him. Tell him that you're going to the bar with me tonight. See how long it takes him to show up here to quash that plan."

She purses her lips and then huffs. "Okay, you're right. He probably won't go for that. But that doesn't mean we can't have margaritas on your lunchbreak tomorrow!"

"I have to work after lunch," I say, laughing again.

"Grant will never know," she says and then quickly changes her mind. "Actually, he probably will because I'll end up spilling the beans somehow."

"Exactly. You can't keep a secret to save your life. You have a guilty conscience."

Holly gasps in outrage. "I do not."

"You do, but it's one of the reasons I love you."

"I love you too." She blows me a kiss, making me smile.

I swear, she always knows how to make me feel better. I'm so thankful that I had her this year. I don't know many people who would leave a new baby just to come and check on me, but she did. That's the kind of person she is. I hope I'm half the friend to her that she is to me.

"What client was being a jerk last night?" she asks.

"Joe Laughlin. He didn't take my advice and lost a million dollars. Now he's pissed off and says it's my fault. He had a meltdown last night." I point at the picture frame still shattered on the floor.

"Holy crap," Holly says. "He did that?"

I nod. "He was completely insane last night."

"Did he hurt you?" Holly growls, her eyes flashing with anger.

"No. I thought he was going to," I admit quietly, shivering at the memory of him backing me into the corner. As angry as I am at Bryant, I'm thankful he was here. As soon as I saw him, I knew I was safe. "Bryant got here in time and threw him out."

"Jesus," Holly whispers, eyes wide. "That's scary, G. You need to tell Grant."

"I plan on it. I was actually planning on going up there after I cleaned up the mess," I say, glancing at the clock. We still have a little time before the morning meeting.

"I should get home," she says. "I promised Ian I wouldn't be gone long."

"He has Finn?"

"Yeah." A bright smile overtakes her face. "He's such a good daddy."

I smile back, thrilled for her. Ian was kind of crazy when she was pregnant. Okay, Ian's always kind of crazy when it comes to Holly, but in the most adorable way ever. He's ridiculously sweet to her. He followed her everywhere when she was pregnant, worried about her and the baby. I don't think he worked a single minute for the entire nine months. It's good to know that falling in love worked out well for one of us.

It certainly didn't for me.

My heart feels like it's been through an industrial grade shedder.

Stupid men.

Stupid Bryant.

Holly climbs to her feet and circles my desk to throw her arms around me in a big hug. "Love you," she says. "Call me if you need me."

"Love you too."

"I mean it, Gia," she says, pulling back to hit me with a stern look. It doesn't really work for her though. She's terrible at being stern. "Call me."

"Okay," I promise anyway. "Kiss Finn for me."

"I will." She lets me go and heads toward the door. "Margaritas soon!"

I shake my head, laughing. She's probably driving Ian and Finn both crazy. She was not made to sit at home. Not even a newborn is enough to slow her down for long.

Once she's gone, I quickly finish cleaning up the mess. Luckily, Mr. Laughlin's tantrum didn't destroy the picture in the frame. It's one of me and my grandma when I was little.

My little sister, Chelsea, was born with spina bifida. She requires a lot of extra care. After my dad died, my mom didn't have time to come to my events and take care of Chelsea. I understood, of course. But Grandma always filled in for her.

I miss her like crazy. She was my hero and my biggest fan before she died. It didn't matter what I was doing, she was always in the first row, cheering me on.

My phone rings before I get all the glass cleaned up.

I carefully drop a shard in the trashcan and then grab my phone.

"This is Gia. How can I help you?"

"Hey, it's Lily."

"Oh, hey," I say. Grant's assistant is also his wife. I love her. She's like sunshine.

"Grant needs to see you," she says.

"Oh, good. I was actually going to call you to see if he was free. I need to talk to him."

"Oh. Is everything okay?"

"I think so," I say, not wanting her to worry. She's the sweetest person I've ever met. She's so soft-hearted and genuinely kind. She's good for Grant too. Makes him think about something other than work. I wasn't here for very long before they met, but I guess he was a workaholic before her.

"Okay. See you in a few minutes," she says and then disconnects.

Lily's on the phone when I step out of the elevator on the top floor a few minutes later, Joe Laughlin's file in hand.

"Go on in," she says, covering the mouthpiece of her phone. She's dressed in an adorable red and white polka-dot dress with a matching bow in her blonde hair. Lily is tiny. I'm also pretty sure she could run this place without breaking a sweat.

"Thank you," I whisper, ducking into Grant's office.

As soon as I'm over the threshold, my gaze collides with Bryant.

He's leaning up against the wall beside Grant's desk, arms crossed over his chest, jaw clenched, those green eyes eating me alive. They scan every inch of me, meticulous in their scrutiny. Even dressed in a well-worn Navy t-shirt and faded blue jeans, he's so damn handsome. He hasn't shaved, so he's scruffy, his jawline wicked sharp.

What's he doing here?

Why does he have to be so damn beautiful?

His eyes lock with mine, something dark and ravenous in them.

I freeze in my tracks, caught in that stare. A pained whimper threatens to escape, but I fight it back, refusing to let him see how much he hurt me. Getting over him would be so much easier if I could forget the way he looks at me like he feels the same powerful connection I do. As if he aches for me as badly as I ache for him. I'm not a small girl.

I'm thick, curvy, and taller than average. But when he looks at me, he makes me feel small and delicate, like something to be treasured.

Even though he broke my heart last night, it keeps crying out for him as if it knows he's the only thing capable of putting it back together again.

Why can't hearts come with a factory reset button?

"Gia," Grant says, looking up from his computer. "Come in."

I stumble forward, tearing my gaze away from Bryant. My heart pounds against my ribcage as if it's fighting to leap out of my chest and into his hands. His hands are rough, but he's so gentle with them. I've dreamed a million times about feeling the rough pads of his fingers gliding down my body, of feeling them grip onto me while he's thrusting inside of me.

No. Bad Gia.

I jerk my mind away from that thought, refusing to go there now. My cheeks feel like they're on fire as I stumble across the room, trying like hell to avoid looking at Bryant again. He always could read me like a book. The last thing I need is for him to know I've been thinking dirty thoughts about him. Wouldn't that be humiliating?

"Bryant was just telling me what happened last night," Grant says when I drop heavily into a chair across from his desk.

Of course that's why he's here. He's such a tattle-tale.

"Bryant should mind his own business," I snap, turning a dark glower on him. He had no right to tell Grant what happened!

His lips quirk up into that crooked smile that makes my heart race. "You are my business, Gia baby," he says, his deep voice almost hypnotic.

Luckily for me, I'm not that easily seduced.

"Don't call me that," I growl. "I am not your business."

"Yeah, you are. You're mine. That makes you my business," he says as if stating a simple fact.

"I am *not* yours. I don't belong to any man, especially not one who doesn't even write me back for a whole year to let me know he's still alive, and then accuses me of sleeping with someone else," I shoot back at him, so mad I want to strangle him.

"Whoa," Grant says, shocked.

Guilt flickers in Bryant's expression before he quickly schools it. Seeing it there doesn't give me any satisfaction. It just makes me feel...sad.

He clenches his jaw but doesn't try to dispute me this time.

"What happened last night, Gia?" Grant asks, changing the subject.

"Joe Laughlin showed up right as we were closing," I explain, turning in my chair so I don't have to see Bryant. "I told Lauren to go ahead and send him up. He's always been a bit of a pompous jackass, but he's never been violent or anything of that nature."

Bryant grunts, shifting around impatiently.

I ignore him. "Last night was different. I think he may be having some sort of mental breakdown," I tell Grant. "He was screaming at me that I lost a million dollars and that he wasn't leaving until I paid it to him. When he came to see me about making this particular investment, I explained to him repeatedly that I had serious concerns, but he insisted I transfer the funds as directed. I had him sign a liability waiver, detailing my concerns and why I had them. I strongly advised against making the investment in my declaration. When I reminded him of all of this, he threw a picture frame at me."

Bryant's angry growl is harder to ignore than his grunt was. It sends chills racing through me, half because the sound is so damn sexy, and half because I think he would have seriously hurt Mr. Laughlin had he seen him throw that picture frame at me. Even if he is a jerk, Bryant is a protector, the kind of guy who would stand up to defend any woman, whether he knew her or not. I know he's a sniper, and that he's killed people before.

Even knowing that, I've never been afraid of him. I've never felt anything less than perfectly safe with him. But I know how much what he does weighs on him sometimes. It would break my heart if he had to live with Mr. Laughlin's death on his conscience too. Bryant may be a jerk, but

I still care about him. I still love him and want the best for him.

I just happen to want to drown him in the bathtub right now too.

Grant's brows pull together, his lips compressing into a grim line. I don't think he's particularly thrilled with Mr. Laughlin. Like Bryant, Grant is protective. He looks out for all of us and has no problem terminating his business relationship with clients who get out of hand. Regardless of how much money they make him, he values people more.

"He missed me," I promise my boss. "But he backed me into a corner. Before he could...do anything to me, Bryant showed up and kicked him out."

"This investment," Grant says. "Was it Elegen?"

I nod.

"They're under federal investigation for wire and securities fraud. Laughlin wasn't merely an investor," Grant says. "He talked countless others in his circle into investing over the last year. If he knew of your concerns before he got involved, he may be facing prison time."

"He knew," I say, flipping open his file. I shuffle through and find the document in question before handing it over to Grant. "The waiver was signed over a year ago. I had Holly witness and Drake notarize it because there was no talking Mr. Laughlin out of investing."

Grant scans the waiver, his expression growing grimmer by the minute. "I'm guessing this is why he lost his fucking mind," he says, passing the document to Bryant. "He knows she has it and he's on the hook."

Bryant scans the document and then gives Grant a curt nod before turning those green eyes on me. "I'm going to be your private security for a while," he announces, sending my world hurtling into orbit.

"No, you're not."

He meets my gaze, his expression stony and resolute. He's serious.

"No, he's not," I say, turning to look at Grant again.

Grant grimaces, holding his hands up. "Surprise?"

"You're kidding me," I whisper, stunned.

"No," Grant says, turning serious again. He holds his hand out for the waiver, which Bryant gives to him. "Laughlin is in deep right now. I'm guessing he's not after the million at all. He wanted access to this file, because his signature on that document could send him to prison for years. He likely hoped that if he pushed hard enough, you'd pull it out and he could get rid of it before anyone else saw it. He's completely off the rails right now."

My eyes widen, a flicker of fear worming its way through me.

"He mentioned the waiver last night," I admit, my stomach roiling. I thought he was out of his mind and that he genuinely didn't remember the waiver, but maybe that's simply what he wanted me to think so I'd give him what he wanted. He knew I had the waiver and wanted it.

He's a smart man. He probably knows that with the documentary evidence rules the way they are, not being able to produce the original would work in his favor. If he can get rid of the original, he might be able to get out of facing charges.

"If he's desperate enough to attack you in your own office, I'm concerned that he may try again," Grant continues, his voice gentle, as if he knows this is not the news I want to hear right now. "Until the FBI picks Laughlin up, you need protection. Bryant is trained to keep people safe."

"Can't someone else do it? Knox? Jason? *Anyone*?"

"No," Bryant growls.

"He's not wrong," Grant says with an apologetic shrug. "I'm turning this over to the FBI today"—he lifts the waiver to indicate what he means—"but we want Laughlin to think you're unaware that he's under investigation. Until he's caught, it's the best way to ensure he doesn't escalate the situation and try something with you that's likely to get his stupid ass killed. The less he thinks you know, the safer you'll be."

Bryant breaks my heart, and I get stuck with him as my babysitter.

Just wonderful.

"Fine, but I don't like it," I mutter, before climbing to my feet. I turn to scowl at Bryant. "Just so we're clear, you are not staying at my house."

"No," he says, his eyes deceptively gentle. "You're staying at mine."

He's definitely lost his mind if he believes that.

"Um, no."

"You're pissed at me," he murmurs, his expression firm and somehow full of understanding at the same time. "And I don't blame you for that, Gia baby. But you will be staying with me, even if I have to carry you."

I glare at him for a second and then storm out of Grant's office.

Lily glances up at me.

"If I search for ways to kill someone on someone else's computer, do you think they can trace it back to me?" I ask her, throwing my hands up in the air.

Lily, sweet, innocent little Lily, doesn't even miss a beat. "I don't know," she says with a shrug. "But if you're talking about Grant, I'll be your alibi."

Chapter Three

Bryant

"**I**F SHE MURDERS ME for this, I'm haunting you," Grant says, looking over at me. He's shaking his head like he doesn't approve, but I see the amusement in his eyes. He thinks Gia giving me hell is hilarious. If it were Lily, he wouldn't find it so funny though. And I know he's as worried about Gia as I am. He's as pissed about what happened last night as I am.

When I called him last night, he was livid. I don't think he's been to sleep since. He's been on the phone with his contacts, trying to run to ground any information on Laughlin he could get his hands on. I'm not thrilled the motherfucker is targeting Gia. Desperate men make desperate choices. He won't have a second opportunity to get close to Gia.

She looks beautiful today, but there's something off about her. She glows when she's happy. She wasn't glowing when she stepped inside this office twenty minutes ago. She looked...defeated. I don't think she slept any better than I did last night. I spent the night parked across from her house, keeping an eye out in case Laughlin decided to try anything. I had to talk myself out of knocking on her door a hundred times.

I fucked up yesterday. Bad. She's going to make me pay for that. And that's fine. After the shit I pulled, I deserve to be frozen out. *She* deserves to know I'll fight for her, no matter what it takes. But right now, her safety takes priority.

She doesn't have to like it. Hell, I won't even ask her to act like she does.

But, make no mistakes about it, her sexy little ass will be sleeping in my house, in my bed tonight. Even if I have to toss her over my shoulder to get her there. I want her where Laughlin will never think to look, where I can keep her safe.

Mischief will help. The dog may be old and mostly blind, but he's still one of the most highly trained dogs to come out of the SEALs in the last decade. And he has a soft spot for women. If anyone gets through me, they won't get through him too, not without a helluva fight.

"You'll survive," I mutter to Grant, pushing away from the wall to go after Gia.

"You might not," he says from behind me, chuckling.

I lift a hand and flip him off. What? He can't fire me since he's technically not my boss. He didn't hire me to protect Gia. I told him the only man in her personal space would be me. He didn't put up a fight. He knows how I feel about her. Not sure how since I tried to keep that shit under wraps until now, but he knows. He also knows I'm more than capable of keeping her safe.

I've helped hunt down and take out men for crimes much more insidious than Laughlin's. I've kept everyone from villagers to royalty safe. It'll take a hell of a lot more than an overweight, desperate millionaire to get through me.

"Good luck!" Grant calls after me.

The fucker. He's changed since I left. He's more laid back, happier. Married life and fatherhood seem to agree with him. Or maybe it's the fact that the little blonde sitting outside his office can't keep her eyes off him. Whatever it is, it's nice to see.

I slip out of his office just in time to see the elevator doors slide shut.

"Fuck."

Lily looks up from her desk and gives me a sympathetic smile. "You might want to give her a little space," she says softly. "She's pretty upset right now."

"I know." Wish like hell I could hold her through it. But considering it's me she's upset with, that'll go over about as well as a screen door on a submarine.

"She's researching ways to get away with murder."

I let out a surprised bark of laughter. If anyone could come up with a foolproof way to get away with killing my big ass, it'd be Gia. She's too goddamn smart for her own good sometimes, and I wouldn't even put up a fight if she tried. Thinking of all the ways she's going to torture me for hurting her should probably worry me. Instead, it has my dick hard. Because I know once she's done being mad, she'll be mine. And there's not a fucking thing in the world stopping me from touching her as often as it takes to soften her up.

Besides, whatever she comes up with probably won't be sufficient. I hurt her badly. I don't think I ever let myself consider how she must have felt for the last year, not hearing from me. I was too afraid if I thought about it, I'd send her my letter, selfishly asking her to wait for me. That wouldn't have been fair to her...at least that's what I told myself.

But she waited for me anyway.

She worried about me anyway.

I don't deserve her, but she's mine anyway.

And nothing is going to stop me from claiming her now. I just left one warzone, but I'll fight another if that's what it takes to win her heart again, to win her trust. I'll fight one to keep her safe too.

Laughlin fucked up last night and targeted the wrong girl. I let him walk out of there alive because I know that's what Gia wanted. If he comes after her again...well, I'm not taking any fucking prisoners this time, that's for damn sure.

"I'll be sure to check my food for poison," I say to Lily, headed toward the stairs. "Thanks for the warning."

"You're welcome," she chirps.

I jog down the stairs, chuckling over the thought of my girl wanting to kill me. Can't say I blame her. If she were anyone else, I wouldn't put up with the attitude, but hers turns me the fuck on like nothing else ever has. My little kitten has claws.

I can't fucking wait to feel them in my skin.

By the time I make it to her floor, she's already rushing toward her office, undoubtedly hoping to avoid me. She has that look about her still, the one that tells me just how badly I fucked up last night. Her eyes are puffy and dull, her lips turned down into a sad frown.

I fucking hate knowing I'm the one who made her look so damn sad.

I lengthen my stride, closing the distance between us quickly. She may have legs for days, but mine are still a helluva lot longer than hers. I'm almost right on top of her when I hear her sniffle. I freeze in my tracks.

She's crying.

Fuck. I made her cry.

My heart plummets toward my stomach.

My entire fucking *soul* cries out in distress.

"Gia baby," I rasp, reaching out for her.

"Don't touch me," she growls, jerking her arm away from me. "You don't get to hurt me and then bully your way back into my life like nothing happened. You broke my heart last night, Bryant. I have nothing to say to you."

"Fuck," I curse, my heart ripping itself into tiny pieces.

She hurries away from me. I stand where I'm at for a long moment, a riptide of emotion swirling through me. I've never seen her like this before. It kills me to know I hurt her so badly she doesn't even want to speak to me. It fucking eviscerates me to know she's crying over me. I don't know how to fix it.

Shit. Can I even fix it?

I have to fix it.

I take off after her, not willing to let her go that easily.

Her door is closed by the time I make it to her office. I tap once and then push it open. She's on the far side of her desk, her head bent. The office is spotless, wiped clean of any evidence of what happened here last night.

She sighs heavily when the door clicks closed behind me.

"I was an asshole last night," I say, keeping my distance so I don't crowd her. "I know I was, Gia baby. And I'm sorry. I never should have jumped to conclusions or treated you like I did. I won't make excuses for it. There are none. I was an asshole."

"Yeah, you were," she says, not bending an inch.

"You have every right to be pissed. I won't try to stop you," I tell her, shoving my hands into my pockets. Around her, the only way I can keep them off her is to keep them put away. It's been that way since the day I met her. "I'll work like a fucking dog to earn your forgiveness, baby. But while I do that, I need you to let me do my job here. I need you to let me keep you safe."

"Why?" she asks, lifting her head to look at me. Even with her mascara smudged and her eyes red, she's devastatingly beautiful. My heart actually fucking aches when those multicolored eyes meet mine. "You didn't care enough to even let me know you were alive. Why do you care now?"

"I always cared," I say, frustrated that she doesn't know it, doesn't see it.

"You have a funny way of showing it," she mutters, fire snapping in her gaze.

"I didn't..."

"What? Want to be bothered?"

"I didn't want you to know how fucking miserable I was without you," I growl, the words ripped from deep within my chest. "Every goddamn day, I missed you, Gia. Every goddamn minute I was gone, I thought about you. Not being here with you tore me up inside. I didn't want to put you through the same thing."

Those eyes widen in shock. She stares at me for a long moment, completely speechless. And then she sighs. "You put me through it anyway, Bryant," she says, her voice soft. Tears shine in her eyes. "I worried about you every day anyway. Worse, I think. Because I didn't know if you were dead or alive. I spent hours poring over every news story I could get my hands on, praying I didn't see your name listed among the dead."

Jesus.

"I'm so fucking sorry, Gia."

She takes a deep breath and then exhales. "It doesn't even matter anymore."

"It does."

"No," she says, shaking her head. "It doesn't. You were in a war. I forgive you for not considering me while you were gone. But you made what you think about me crystal clear last night. You accused me of being a cheater, and you made me feel like writing you was wrong. If you insist on keeping me safe, then fine. I'll be civil. But we're not friends, Bryant. Not anymore."

"The hell we aren't," I growl, striding across the room toward her.

"Back up," she says, a tremor in her voice.

I don't listen. Of course I don't. I stalk her like a fucking animal, step for step. Until she's pressed against the filing cabinet, her tits heaving in her pretty green blouse. I step up in front of her, so close I can feel the silky fabric shift against my hand with every exhalation, smell her intoxicating blackberry and jasmine scent swirling around us.

It's a dangerous line to walk after what happened last night. But I'm not Laughlin. She may be angry at me right now, but she knows I would never lay a hand on her...that I'd kill anyone who did. Even if she hates me, she knows I'll keep her safe.

"We're going to be more than friends real soon, Gia baby," I growl, tipping her chin up slightly, forcing her to look at me. Her eyes are glazed, her cheeks flushed. As expected, she's not afraid. She's turned on. My heart leaps, allowing me to pull in my first deep breath since I saw the tears on her cheeks. "As soon as you forgive me, I'm claiming what's always been mine."

"What..." She stops and licks her lips. "W-what's always been yours?"

"This," I say, reaching out to lay my hand over her heart. It hammers wildly beneath my palm, racing away from her. I slide my hand down her body, feeling the way her soft stomach quivers beneath my palm. I dip my hand between her legs, cupping her center possessively. "And this."

"Bryant," she whimpers.

I want to kiss her, more desperately than I think I've ever wanted anything. But I know her as well now as I did a year ago. I know that tremor in her voice isn't merely desire. It's worry, unease...hesitation. She wants me, as badly as I want her. But she doesn't trust me to guard her heart right now. She isn't ready right now.

When I kiss her, she will be. Not just for that kiss, but for me. For us.

"Fight me, Gia baby," I murmur. "Fight like hell if you need to do it. Hate me if that makes you feel better. I'll carry that for you. I'll carry whatever you need me to carry. But know that when you're done being mad, you're mine." I release her and then, because I'm a glutton for punishment and I can't help myself, I lean forward and press my lips to the soft plane of her cheek. "You've always been mine, pretty baby."

"Bryant," she whispers, pleading this time.

I take a step back, giving her room.

"I'll be right outside if you need anything," I say, knowing I need to give her time to process what just happened. I also know if I don't warn her that I'll be out there, she may very well try to run. That won't end well for either of us. I can deal with her anger. I won't deal with her putting herself in danger just to piss me off. And right now, my girl looks like she's tempted to flee.

"Are you going to pout or are you going to eat?" I ask, quirking my brow at Gia from across the table. We're at Noni's. She's mad as hell I invited myself to lunch with her. If looks could kill, I'd definitely be burning in hell right now. Her adorable scowl is doing a number on my cock. She stayed in her office all morning, not even poking so much as a toe outside.

Ms. Janice brought me a chair after she walked by for the third time and saw me standing out there. She didn't ask any questions. She just rolled a chair out to me, shook her head, said welcome home, and went about her business. I like her. Nothing fazes her. She keeps Davis Financial running like a well-oiled machine.

When Gia finally left her office for lunch, she'd rebuilt all those walls I broke down this morning. She's still mad as hell. It's fucking adorable...not that I'm telling her that shit anytime soon. Are you kidding me? I may be an idiot, but I'm not crazy.

I'm also pretty sure she really would poison my food if she thought she could get away with it. Luckily, I know her well enough to know she doesn't have a mean bone in her body. She might want to poison me, but she's too gentle to actually do it. The girl can't even kill spiders, and she's terrified of them. She read me the riot act the first time she called me for help because there was a spider in her kitchen, and I tried to kill it.

Apparently, my role as her hero involved putting the spider outside, not squishing it. She lectured me about how important spiders are to the terrestrial ecosystem, whatever the fuck that means. I let her ramble on though, fantasizing about bending her over the counter and eating her from behind while she talked.

"I'm not pouting," she lies, stabbing her fork into her salad. She takes an exaggerated bite, giving me a dirty look the entire time.

I just grin at her, amused. "You're beautiful all the time, but you're fucking adorable when you're pissed, Gia baby."

She chews her bite and then dabs at her mouth with her napkin. "Stop calling me that," she says. "I don't like it."

"You do, but I'll let you pretend you don't, kitten."

Those pretty eyes narrow on me. And then, thank God, the ice cracks. A tiny smile tugs at the corners of her lips. "You're such a pain in the ass, Bryant."

"It's one of the things you always liked best about me," I remind her, pushing her pizza closer to her. She doesn't eat enough.

"You were gone a long time."

"Thirteen months."

"It felt longer," she whispers. Her gaze drifts from me to the advertisements placed beneath the glass of the table.

"Yeah, it did," I say, my voice soft. "I hated when you stopped writing me."

"I wasn't sure if you would be there to get my letters," she mumbles, with a shrug. "I knew you would be coming home soon, but I didn't know exactly when."

"I should have told you."

She shrugs again. I expect her to ask why I never wrote her, but she doesn't.

"Am I allowed to ask about your time over there?" she says instead.

"You can ask me anything," I murmur, hating how unsure she sounds. I don't want to tell her about the shit I saw and did over there. Things like war and death and the screams of the dying and sobs of the living don't belong in her life. But if she wants to know, I'll tell her. I don't want any secrets between us.

She lifts her gaze to mine again, scrutinizing my expression, looking for any hint that I'm not being honest with her. Whatever she sees there seems to settle her. "What was it like?" she finally asks, relaxing slightly. "I read a lot about what was going on over there. It seems so...sad."

"It is sad," I agree and then nod at her pizza. "Eat, baby."

She doesn't fight me this time. She picks up a slice of pizza and takes a bite.

"Syria is in the middle of a civil war, with civilians fighting to overthrow ISIL, who controls the nation's government. Most of what we did is classified, but we spent a lot of time training the rebels, teaching them what they needed to know to take Syria back from ISIL," I murmur, grabbing parmesan to sprinkle on my pizza. "We also evacuated civilians ahead of airstrikes and safeguarded the oil fields for the SDF."

"Oh," she says. "Were you in combat?"

"Occasionally." I take a bite of my pizza and then chew before continuing, "We were called on to take out several targets. Mostly mid-rank ISIL members, a couple higher ranking ones. I'm not supposed to talk about it, but I'll tell you everything if you want to know."

"You don't have to do that. I don't want you to get in trouble." She shrugs like she's uncomfortable. "I just worried about you. So many people have died over there."

"Most of our time was spent training SDF forces and rescuing civilians," I promise her. It sounds easier than it was. The entire region is a quagmire of international crises and conflicts waiting to happen. With Turkey and Russia heavily involved in helping ISIL, and most of the rest of the world opposed, things were tense from word one. And ISIL is a hell of a lot less careful about protecting innocent lives than the coalition forces have been.

There's a reason millions of people have fled, more willing to leave behind everything they know and live in refugee camps than spend another minute under the thumb of ISIL. What's happening over there isn't merely sad. It's a goddamn tragedy that's been dragging on for years.

"Oh," Gia says again, and then takes several bites, chewing while she thinks. "Will you have to go back?"

"No. This tour was my last."

She blinks at me.

"I'm out now."

"Seriously? You quit?"

"You don't quit the Navy," I tease, grinning at her. "My contract was up. I opted not to reenlist."

"What? Why?" she asks, staring at me in complete shock.

"It was time, Gia baby," I murmur, meeting her gaze, willing her to see the truth...that I walked away for her. Because I couldn't put either of us through another deployment. Because I'm so fucking in love with her the thought of leaving her again is actual torture. And because I'm tired of living that life, of finding new, more fucked up memories to replace the older ones. War doesn't get easier. You just become numb to the horrors of it. But once the fighting is done, those memories start to leak out. If you're lucky, that's all they ever do. If you're not, they consume you.

PTSD is a motherfucker. I already skirt that line, carefully balancing what I've done for God and country on a scale that tips more wildly with every deployment. I don't need another one to upend the scale completely. I've been fortunate so far. I'd rather not tempt fate by hoping my luck continues to hold.

"What are you going to do now?" she asks, averting her gaze as if she's afraid to face the truth of what's happening between us just yet. And as frustrating as that is for me...I can't blame her for it. I still have a lot of work to do to win her back. "Are you coming back to work?"

"Not sure," I admit before taking another bite. "I've been toying with the idea of going into personal security."

"You're not nearly as funny as you think you are," she says, scowling at me.

I chuckle, shaking my head. "I'm serious, Gia baby. It's good money and this is Tennessee. There are country stars everywhere in need of a little muscle to make sure everyone minds their p's and q's."

"You'd be good at it," she mutters after a moment, her tone grudging. "You're big enough."

"You like how big I am, baby?"

"No." She rolls her eyes at me. Her blush gives her away though.

Huh. Seems I'm not the only one whose been fantasizing.

"You will," I promise her, my voice a gritty scrap of sound.

Her blush deepens before she drops her gaze to her food.

We eat in silence for a few minutes. She's more relaxed than she was when we got here, more like herself, only a little quieter than normal. I miss her chatter. I could listen to her all day every day and never grow bored. She has a way of surprising me with the shit that comes out of her mouth. She drops knowledge like bombs.

"Why is Dante staying with you?" I finally ask, desperate to hear her voice again.

"He was visiting Vanderbilt," she says, dabbing at her mouth again. "They've been recruiting him pretty hard this year."

"Shit. I forgot he's graduating."

"He's eighteen," she says, her voice soft. Even though her siblings are younger than she is, they've always been close. I never met Dante, but she talked about him a lot. He's a hell of a tight end. She's incredibly proud of him.

I feel bad for being a dick to him yesterday. In my defense, they look nothing alike. And he doesn't look like any eighteen-year-old kid I've ever met. He's big. I thought he was closer to Gia's age than a teenager. I'm guessing winning him over is going to take some work after the shitshow I directed yesterday.

"He wants to play for Vanderbilt?" I ask.

"He wants to be close to home," she says with an annoyed shake of her head. "He worries about me, Chelsea, and mom too much."

"You're worth worrying about, Gia baby."

"Don't," she whispers.

"Don't what?"

"Don't make me think you care about me if you don't, Bryant," she whispers, her voice thin, almost pleading. "Don't give me hope if you don't mean it."

"Fuck," I rumble and then slide out of the booth. I circle the table and then kneel beside her, reaching out to tip her chin so she's looking at me. She resists for a split second before giving in. Her eyes meet mine, wide and full of worry. "I'm not playing a game with you, Gia. The last thing I want to do is hurt you again."

"I want to believe you." I hear the yearning in her voice, the fragile hope.

"You will," I promise, brushing my thumb over her soft bottom lip. "When you let me in again, you'll never again have a reason to doubt me."

I don't know if she believes me, but her expression softens slightly. For now, it's enough.

Chapter Four

Gia

"YOU'RE STAYING WITH ME," Bryant growls, glaring at me over the top of my car. How he manages to look hot when he's pissed off, I don't know, but he does. He's been outside my office all day, sitting there like he really expects Mr. Laughlin to show up in the middle of the day. He's crazy.

Trying to remember that I'm angry at him is a lot of work. I want, so badly, to believe him when he says I'm his, but the sting from yesterday lingers, making me hesitant to trust him. He might not know it, but he's the only person in the world with the power to completely break me. Before last night, I never even considered that he might do it. But he hurt me yesterday. More than I ever imagined he would.

And now he's determined to make me crazy on top of it.

"I want to stay at my own house," I growl at him, refusing to give up that easily. If he and Grant think I need to be protected, then fine. I'll let him follow me around like he's guarding the Pope. But he can do that while I sleep in my own bed.

"It's too exposed."

"I live on a cul-de-sac!"

"Exactly. That means there's only one way out," he says. "If he comes for you, where are you going to go?"

"I..." I hesitate for a split second before ingenuity strikes. "He doesn't know where I live. He can't come for me without my address."

"What if he followed you home last night?"

"I..." My hesitation lasts longer this time, a chill working its way through me. I didn't consider that. "He didn't follow me home. I would have noticed," I finally say, though I can hear the thread of uncertainty in my voice. Which means he can too.

"You think so?" Bryant cocks his head to the side. "Did you notice that I followed you home, Gia baby? Or that I sat outside your house all night to make sure he didn't show up?"

"What?" I blink at him. "You did not."

"I did."

My heart sinks when I realize he's not joking. He really did follow me home. I didn't have a clue. That's probably not a good thing considering Mr. Laughlin has gone off the deep end. What if he'd been the one to follow me? Dante was there last night, but he won't be tonight. He's headed back to Atlanta. I'll be completely alone.

Another chill rips through me. This one freezes me from the inside out.

"You done arguing with me now?" Bryant asks, though his tone is gentle.

I nod, dismayed.

He sighs softly and then circles around to me. Before I can say or do anything, he's got his arms around me, pulling me up against the hard wall of his chest. "Don't be afraid," he whispers, the demand gritty. "You're perfectly safe with me. I won't let anything happen to you, Gia baby."

I stand rigid in his arms for a long moment, trying desperately to resist how badly I want to be in them. How much I want to stay in them. And then I give up fighting it and let him hold me. He keeps me close, curling his big body around mine as if he intends to use his size to block out the rest of the world for me.

"Don't let this change the way you view the world," he says. "You need to believe the best of people, and the world needs you to believe it too. Don't let that change because you're afraid."

I lay my head on his shoulder, wrapping my arms around his waist. His body is rock hard, comprised of bulky muscle. He smells so damn good, like spring rain and safety. Tears sting at my eyes at how carefully he holds me. My heart pulses, aching for him. His hammers against my arm, pounding a steady, soothing rhythm.

"I'd take a bullet before I let him close to you. So long as I knew you were safe, I'd die happy," he murmurs, his voice pitched low, as if he doesn't intend to say it out loud but can't quite help himself. He means every word. I hear the truth vibrating in his voice, feel it seeping into me.

I don't know why he never wrote me, but it wasn't because he didn't care. I can't pretend anymore that it was.

The last of my anger evaporates, vanishing.

"I'll stay with you," I whisper.

His lips brush my forehead in a featherlight kiss.

We stay there for a long time, just holding each other. And then I hear the elevator ding. Voices spill out a moment later, coworkers headed toward their vehicles. Bryant curses beneath his breath and reluctantly releases me.

"I'll follow you to your house to get your shit," he says.

"Stuff."

He looks at me sideways.

"Stop calling it my shit. It's my stuff."

His lips quirk. "Get your cute ass in the car, baby."

I huff and then sail past him to my car.

His quiet laughter chases after me.

"Jerk," I mumble, though I feel my lips twitch too.

I missed him so damn much. He always loved to rile me up and tease me. Our friendship was full of laughter and playful moments. When I was with him, I was always so freaking happy. He lit me up like the sun, setting me ablaze. I've missed laughing with him.

Once he's in his truck, I back out of my spot and head toward my house. I turn the radio to my favorite station and sing along, trying to quiet the tangled roar of my mind. It races a thousand miles a minute, trying to sort through the emotional turmoil of the last twenty-four hours. I don't know how to make sense of it though because I still don't understand why he didn't write me back.

He says I'm his, but what does that mean exactly? That he wants to be with me? Fuck me? That he's as hopelessly in love with me as I am with him? I want to believe it's the latter. Desperately. But if I'm wrong...what? We become friends again? I spend the rest of my life wishing for more?

"Why is love so complicated?" I cry out into my empty car, frustrated that I can't make sense of it. My mind is analytical. It needs order and answers and logical thought processes. There's nothing logical or ordered about love, though. It's all emotion and intuition and instinct. I don't understand any of it.

But I do know there's no way I can just be Bryant's friend. I was deluding myself to ever think I could carry on with just his friendship. I can't. It will break me every day.

And, as I've discovered in the last twenty-four hours, I'm not particularly good at being broken.

The drive to my house takes about half an hour because of traffic. I anxiously check my rearview mirror every few minutes to make sure Bryant's still behind me. He is, with his eyes locked on my car like he's hyper-focused on it.

Butterflies kick into flight in my stomach.

I pull into my driveway, taking deep breaths in an attempt to calm myself. And then I notice that something's wrong. My front door is cracked open. I locked it this morning when Dante and I left. I'm absolutely certain of that fact.

Someone's been inside my house.

My phone rings, startling me.

I let out a squeak and then grab my phone from my purse. Bryant's name flashes across the screen. I scramble to turn the radio down and answer.

"Someone's been inside the house," I blurt as soon as I put the phone to my ear.

"Stay inside your car with the doors locked," he orders me.

"Okay," I agree. I may be headstrong, but I'm not an idiot. If someone is in my house, they didn't come here to have tea and make small talk. They're here for me...maybe to hurt me, definitely to scare me.

I watch in the rearview mirror as Bryant pulls up at the curb, leaving me room to back out in case I need to flee.

He leans over toward the passenger seat for a moment and then slides out of the truck. I whimper when I see the gun in his hands, fear quaking through me. Not for myself, but for him. He plans on going inside. What if someone is still in there? What if they hurt him?

I know he knows how to handle a gun—this is the south, and he was a freaking sniper. But I still worry about him. This isn't Syria or Iraq or any of the places he's been in recent years. This is Chattanooga. His home. If he has to shoot someone here, it won't be because he was at war.

"Shh, baby," he croons into the phone, his voice gentle like rain. "You're going to be safe, all right? I made a promise to you and I'm not going to break it now."

"Bryant," I whisper, wanting to tell him that I love him. That I'm sorry I've been so angry at him today. That I forgive him and just want him to be safe. But he doesn't give me a chance to say any of those things.

"Stay in your car, Gia," he says. "And call 911."

Before I can agree, he disconnects, confident I'll do as instructed. I hit the locks on my car and then dial 911. My hands shake so badly it takes two tries before I manage to get the simple number in there correctly. I watch him the whole time, sending up a litany of silent prayers that no one is inside.

He moves with such grace, such ease. He's like a lion stalking its prey, every single movement intentional and somehow instinctive at the same time. I've never noticed before just how damn confident he is, like he knows that, regardless of what's going on inside my house, he'll be the one walking out safely.

It gives me the confidence I need to quickly relay the situation to the 911 dispatcher. She's calm, her soothing voice giving me something to focus on beyond the wild thunder of my heart.

"Tell your friend not to go inside and let the police handle it," she says.

Yeah, right. No one tells Bryant what to do. I'm pretty sure it would take me and a whole army to keep him from going inside to check out the situation.

"He's a Navy SEAL," I mutter. Well, he was. Now, he's...what exactly? Retired? I don't know. I'm also still not sure why he didn't enter into a new contract. Was it because of me? Did he think I would want him to quit? I would *never* ask him to choose between me and his job.

"Oh." The dispatcher seems relieved to hear that he's a SEAL. She promises me that help is coming, and then asks me to stay on the line with her to keep her updated about the situation.

Bryant disappears through the front door.

My heart goes with him.

The dispatcher keeps me talking, asking me a thousand questions. I quickly fill her in on the situation with Mr. Laughlin. I'm not sure if I'm supposed to keep that to myself, but I don't see a way to avoid telling her about him since she works for the police.

Grant turned over the waiver documents to the FBI this morning. He said they might have questions for me later, that I might need to make a statement. I agreed, of course. Until last night, I didn't have anything against Mr. Laughlin. I'm used to dealing with arrogant, entitled millionaires. It's what I do every day. But if he helped his friend deceive and defraud others, he deserves to go to jail.

I sob with relief when Bryant appears in the doorway again. My gaze roves over him, checking to make sure he's not hurt. His eyes come to me instantly. He's on his phone, but he heads my way.

"What's happening, Gia?" the 911 dispatcher asks.

"He's outside. B-bryant," I tell her. "He's safe."

"Good. That's very good. Can I speak to him?"

"Um, yes." I quickly throw my door open and climb from the car on trembling legs. I'm barely on my feet before Bryant has his arms around me, pulling me close and holding me tight. I cling to him like my life depends on it.

"I'm here," he murmurs, his lips at my ear. "I've got you."

"T-the dispatcher wants to t-talk to you," I manage to tell him before holding my phone out to him. My teeth chatter. Even though it's warm out, I feel cold, the kind that seeps all the way into your bones.

"Grant, I'll call you back," Bryant says into his phone before taking mine.

I bury my face in his throat and let him hold me as he explains to the dispatcher that he checked the house over. Everything is a mess, and he doesn't know if anything was taken, but there's no one inside. By the time he finishes talking to her, I hear sirens in the distance.

He disconnects and shoves my phone in his pocket.

"You're shaking, Gia baby," he murmurs, rubbing his hands up and down my arms to warm me up.

"I t-thought something was going to happen to you," I admit, rubbing my face on his shirt like that's going to stop him from noticing that I've been crying. I probably have mascara all over my face. It's definitely smeared on the shoulder of his shirt.

"Hey." He tucks his thumb and forefinger under my chin, forcing me to look at him. His expression is soft. There are over one hundred and seventy thousand words currently in use in the English language. Not one of them comes close to describing the emotion and promise blazing like emerald suns in his eyes. "I just spent a year in hell without you. Not a fucking thing on this earth is going to take me away from you now. I'm not going anywhere, Gia baby. Certainly not before I convince you to fall in love with me."

"Bryant," I whisper, my heart and stomach both leaping so high it feels like when my mom would take little hills at a high rate of speed when I was a kid...like my insides are turning somersaults.

He presses his lips to mine in a fleeting kiss as a patrol car comes into view. His lips are soft against mine and gone far too soon.

"Let's deal with this shit, and then we'll talk," he mutters, using his thumbs to wipe away the evidence of my tears.

"Okay," I agree, feeling hopeful for the first time since he broke my heart last night.

By the time the police take my statement and I walk through the house, trying to sort out if anything was taken, I'm drained. As far as I can tell, nothing is missing. But whoever broke in—and there is only one suspect: Mr. Laughlin—prowled through all of my belongings, over-turning drawers and my file cabinet. My dresser drawers are open, my undergarments spilling out onto the floor.

My skin crawls at the thought of Mr. Laughlin going through my underwear, touching them, seeing where I sleep. My house isn't large. It's a single-story two bedroom on a cul-de-sac in the center of a middle-class neighbor-hood full of families. The house has always felt safe to me.

Bryant remains at my side the entire time I make my way through the house, but even with his calming presence, the house no longer feels like home. It no longer feels safe. Mr.

Laughlin didn't even have to damage the door to get in. He picked the lock.

Grant shows up right as the police are getting ready to leave.

"Are you okay?" he asks, striding across the room to hug me.

"Yeah," I mumble, not sure what else I'm supposed to say.

"We're going to find this motherfucker," he promises me before squeezing me tight and then releasing me. He glances around the room, taking in the mess. His jaw tics, his blue eyes glittering with anger. "He won't have another chance."

I nod, feeling a little numb.

"Pack your stuff, Gia baby," Bryant says and then kisses me on the forehead before stepping out into the hall to talk to Grant. "We'll be right out here."

I stand there for a moment, just looking at the mess. I hear Bryant and Grant murmuring back and forth but can't make out what they're saying. I don't think they want me to know. Normally, that would piss me off. I'm a grown woman, more than capable of actively participating in a conversation that impacts my life. But right now, I'm not angry or annoyed about being left out of it. I think I might actually be...grateful.

I'm too tired to deal with anything else.

Shaking my head, I force myself to get moving. I grab all of the underwear and bras that are on the floor and then hesitate. Instead of tossing them back in the drawer or in the laundry basket, I dump them in the trashcan beside my bed. I don't want anything against my naked body that Mr. Laughlin touched.

I straighten the other drawers, grabbing a handful of stuff to throw into a bag to take to Bryant's house. Since I have to work for the rest of the week, I also grab several outfits out of the closet. I don't know how long I'll be at Bryant's. Forever doesn't seem long enough anymore.

Once that's done, I make my way into the bathroom to gather my toiletries. Unlike the rest of the house, the bathrooms are untouched. I sweep everything I need off the shelf into a toiletry bag, toss my mascara, blush, and lipstick in there with it, and then pause when I catch sight of my reflection in the mirror.

Traces of the mascara Bryant wiped away remain. I quickly finish wiping them off, trying to put myself back into order. I feel like a naïve little girl. Even though I knew the situation was serious, I didn't really believe that Mr. Laughlin was dangerous or that he'd keep coming for me. I guess I thought the police would arrest him and my life would go right back to normal, with nothing more than a shattered picture frame to remind me of his tantrum.

Clearly, I was wrong.

I can't help but think that wasn't the only thing I've been wrong about lately. Like Bryant. Holly tried to tell me that he acted the way he did last night out of jealousy, but I refused to even consider it. I'm not so sure she was wrong now, though. Whatever his reason for not writing me, I can't even pretend to be angry at him anymore, not when the only thing in the world I want right now is to feel his arms around me.

He said he wants me to fall in love with him. I'm already there. I fell like a star plummeting to earth, gaining speed as I went. I didn't break apart when I entered the atmosphere though. I left a mile-wide path in my wake. My whole world changed when I fell for him, and it hasn't been the same since.

I don't want it to be. I've always played it safe, did the logical thing. With Bryant, I want to leap before I look. In my heart of hearts, I think I've always known that he would be there to catch me...and not because he's my friend. But because he loves me as much as I love him. Because he's always loved me, intensely, passionately...powerfully.

"Hey," I whisper, catching his reflection in the mirror as he steps into the bathroom behind me.

He doesn't say anything. Instead, he steps up behind me, pressing his body flush to mine. One arm goes around my waist, pulling me backward into his little bubble. His gaze roves over my face in the mirror, scrutinizing me again, searching.

He does that a lot...looks at me as if he's reading his favorite book.

"You okay?" he asks, tipping his head forward slightly. His nose slides along the crown of my head, trailing toward my ear. He inhales deeply as if trying to hold my scent in his lungs, make it part of him.

"Yeah," I whisper, tilting my head to the side to place a kiss on his pec. I never noticed before how good we look together. I'm not small, but he isn't either. He's a solid wall of muscle, firm and unyielding. He's hard to my soft, fierce to my gentle. We look like we belong together.

"You ready?" he asks, splaying his hand across my abdomen. Warmth flows through me, spreading outward from that point of contact. I feel it deep in my womb, and then somewhere deeper. My heart or soul or whatever part of me it is that recognizes the same part of him.

I've always been attracted to him, always wanted him so acutely it makes me ache. Somehow, I feel it even more strongly in this moment. Feel him more deeply. He's not asking if I'm ready to leave. He's asking if I'm ready for this, for us, for him. If I'm ready to become his in all ways, permanently, unalterably. Forever.

"Yes," I whisper, the only possible answer I could give.

Chapter Five

Bryant

"H EY, BUDDY," GIA CROONS, dropping to her knees just inside my front door, heedless of her skirt and heels. She holds her hand out for Mischief, who sniffs her out in exactly zero point two seconds. He goes straight for her, his tail extended, swishing back and forth. Gia lets him smell her before sinking her hands into his thick fur to pet him. "What's his name?"

"Mischief," I murmur to her, my heart warming at the sight of her cooing over him.

He laps up the attention, greedy for affection. He's always been that way. When he's working, he's a beast, capable of tearing a man apart if given the command. But when he's not in work mode, he's as docile as they come, cleverly finding new ways to get the attention he loves.

"Hi, Mischief," Gia says, laughing quietly when he accidentally knocks her backward. She lands on her bottom and stretches her legs out for him. He crawls on top of her, laying his head on her shoulder. She doesn't seem to mind.

"He's mostly blind," I tell her, locking the door and setting the alarm. "Don't let him fool you though. He's still more than capable of causing all sorts of mischief." He's always been that way. He's part Border Collie, part Akita. Border Collies and Akitas are incredibly intelligent breeds, and Mischief might just be one of the smartest. Most dogs that deploy with the troops have one job. They deliver messages or help with recon. They stand guard or track. They do search and rescue or sniff out IEDs and bombs. Mischief could do them all and was determined as hell to prove it. I must have left him at base a hundred times during the early days, only for him to chase after us every time.

He's been with me for almost a decade now. When he started losing his sight on this last deployment, the vet suggested I put him down. The hell with that though. He may not be able to see the world clearly anymore, but that doesn't mean he isn't capable of experiencing the world. Luckily, my chain of command agreed. He's retired like me now. He'll live out the rest of his days here.

"I didn't know you had a dog," she says, laughing when he flops over on her lap for her to scratch his belly. His tail beats the floor a thousand miles a minute, his tongue lolling out.

"He's a military dog, a work dog," I explain, stepping around her to place her bag near the stairs. "He was embedded with my team. He started losing his sight not long after we made it to Syria. By the time our deployment ended, he was almost completely blind."

"Aww, poor guy," she murmurs, melting for him.

"He's retired now, but don't let that fool you," I warn her. "If anyone gets through me, I guarantee they won't get through him. He'll protect you with his life."

"Oh," she whispers, her gaze shifting from me to him again. She processes that for a moment and then smiles at him. "So you're my new hero, huh, big guy?"

"Mischief, *ke mne.*"

He rolls to his feet and pads to my side.

"*Hodny,*" I praise him, rubbing his head. "Gia, come here, baby." I hold out a hand to help her to her feet. She flashes those long legs at me as she rises, making my back teeth ache again. If I don't make love to her soon, I'm going to lose my damn mind.

Once she's standing beside me, I place her hand in front of Mischief so he can smell her.

"Mischief, *pozor,*" I tell him.

He instantly goes on alert, baring his back teeth and growling as he positions himself in front of Gia, his fur standing up between his shoulders.

Gia startles slightly.

"It's okay," I tell her. "I told him to guard you. When I give that command, he'll put himself between you and anything that threatens you. If you use it, he won't let up until he's commanded to stop, understood?"

"*Pozor* is the word?" she asks.

"Yes."

"I understand," she says, her voice solemn. And I know she does. Even if someone comes after her, she'll remember the word. She forgets nothing.

"*Volno*," I murmur to Mischief, giving him the command to relax.

He growls a final time and then plops down, butting Gia with his head for scratches.

"Good boy," she says, seeming to know what he wants. She rubs his ears and the top of his head, praising him. "You're such a good guard dog, Mischief."

I let her love on him for a minute and then slip my hand into hers, tugging to get her moving. She glances around as we walk through the house, her eyes wide as she takes it in. I live on Signal Mountain, tucked as far back into the hills as I can get. My house isn't large, but it's mine. I built it with my own hands. It took me years to finish it.

The house is a log cabin, with a big porch that runs the entire length of the front and large bay windows. The living room sits to the left of the entryway, with the stairs to the right. Through the living room is the kitchen, with a dining room off to the side. My office is on the opposite side. The upstairs landing looks down on the living room, with the master suite to the left and three bedrooms to the right.

When I built it, I wasn't sure why I wanted so many bedrooms when it was just me. Seeing Gia here though, watching her face light up as she examines the house...I realize this is what I subconsciously wanted even then. Her. A family. Someone to share my life with. I didn't know her when I started building the place, but part of me longed for her anyway. Part of me was preparing for her anyway.

"You really built this place?" she asks, turning in a circle in the middle of the living room. Mischief sits beside me, his face turned in her direction too. Even though he can't see her well, I think he feels her over there. I think he's already in love with her.

God knows, it didn't take me long to fall. Somewhere between looking into her beautiful eyes for the first time, and her asking me for my name, my heart landed at her feet. It's been hers every second since.

"Yeah," I say, my dick throbbing in time to my heart. Seeing her here...Jesus. I must have wished for this shit every day for the six months I knew her before I deployed. The reality is even better. She looks at home, like she belongs exactly where she's at, turning in circles in the middle of my living room with her hair dancing around her face.

"It's beautiful, Bryant," she says, giving me that sweet smile that haunts my dreams.

"Not nearly as beautiful as you are, Gia baby," I say. It sounds like a line, but it isn't. It's simple truth. The house may be gorgeous, but it pales in comparison to the star shining in front of me. She's so goddamn perfect. I'll never understand why no one has claimed her before now, but I'm damn glad no one has tried. She's mine. Yesterday, today, tomorrow. Forever.

She stops spinning in circles and turns to face me. The look in her eyes cinches my balls up tight. I don't know when she forgave me or why, but there's no anger or distrust in her gaze now. There's no hesitation or fear. There's just her and those beautiful multicolored eyes, stripping me bare, consuming me whole.

"Come on," I say, holding my hand out to her again. "Let me make you dinner."

"You don't have to do that," she says sweetly, shyly. She slips her hand into mine though, letting me lead her to the kitchen.

I sit her down at the island, and then, because I can't resist, I sweep her hair to the side and place my lips against her neck. Her skin is so fucking soft. I inhale her scent, letting it settle a little of the residual rage still working through me. It's been there since the instant I realized someone had been inside her house.

A soft sigh escapes her lips, her body trembling.

I back off before I end up having her for dinner. She settles in at the island while I prowl through the freezer, looking for something to make her. There's not a lot to choose from. I stopped at the store only long enough to pick up the necessities for me and Mischief. Thankfully, I have the shit I need to make spaghetti.

Mischief sticks a paw in his bowl and drags it across the room toward Gia, which makes her laugh in delight. Now that he knows guarding her is his job, he won't leave her side for long. Once he's close enough for his satisfaction, he sits and starts to eat. I leave food in the bowl so he can eat when he wants. There's also a doggie door for him so he can let himself in and out. He may be mostly blind, but he knows every inch of this property. He guards it when I'm not around, though there isn't a whole lot to guard against way out here. Mostly, he just lays out in the sun and basks.

"Do you think they'll find Laughlin soon?" Gia asks as I set to work on the spaghetti.

I certainly fucking hope they find the fucker soon. Seeing her afraid is intolerable to me. Knowing that motherfucker broke into her house and rifled through her belongings...I almost hoped he was still inside today. He wouldn't have walked out.

She doesn't know it, but we left her car at her place in the hopes he'd return. Grant has Jason and Knox sitting on the place. Chattanooga has one of their guys sitting on the house too. If he shows up again, we'll get him. And I have a feeling he will show up again.

Men like him don't stop until they're stopped. They think they're above the law, entitled to whatever they want. As a sniper, it was my job to prove them wrong. A bullet to the head is an efficient, final lesson. Those who won't stop, get stopped. I'll put a bullet in this fucker's head too if that's what it takes to guarantee Gia's safety.

"Hopefully," I murmur, not wanting to get her hopes up or worry her.

She chatters as I cook, rambling about her day, catching me up on everything that's happened since I left...which is, apparently, a lot. Everyone is married and popping out babies now. It seems to happen at lightning speed, though I'm not surprised.

A lot of men in Grant's position discount women, think they aren't smart enough to do the things he does. Grant knows better. While his competitors cycle through the same talent, he scoops up the analysts others overlook, those who don't fit the stereotypical mold...those who just graduated or are still in school, young women, and people from disadvantaged backgrounds.

If he believes in you, it's because he sees something in you worth believing in. He hires people he genuinely likes. He gives them the tools they need to thrive, and then sits back and lets them do it. I've yet to see him hire the wrong person.

Davis Financial is full of talented young women and the men willing to answer to and support them. Everyone is family, handpicked by Grant to join the fold. It's not hard to see why love makes the rounds as quickly as it does. When you hire people infinitely worthy and capable of love, it's bound to happen.

"Lauren really missed you," Gia says quietly while I strain the noodles.

"I missed her too," I murmur, knowing Gia didn't bring it up out of jealousy. She loves Lauren, and she knows that Lauren is the closest thing to family I have. She's like a little sister to me. From the day I met her, I've had a soft spot for her. I missed her almost as much as I missed Gia, but I know Knox was looking out for her. It took him about two seconds to fall for her. I'm happy for her. She deserves love in her life. Her mother is a straight up bitch, and I don't say that lightly.

"Knox is good for her," she says.

"Yeah, he is." I talked to Lauren and Knox briefly yesterday morning. She looked happy, settled in a way she never did before. And Knox couldn't keep his eyes off her. "What do you want to drink, baby?"

"Um, maybe just tea if you have any."

"I have it," I say, grinning to myself. Gia survives on sweet tea and coffee. I may have only gotten home the day before yesterday, but it was one of the first things I tossed in my shopping cart.

I make her a glass and carry it to her before going back to finish our plates.

"This looks really good, Bryant," Gia says. "I didn't know you could cook."

"I know how to cook." I grin at her. "But you're the next thing to a chef. If the choice is between eating my food and your leftovers, I'm going with yours every time, baby."

She blushes, dropping her eyes to her plate.

We eat in silence for several moments. Well, I eat. Gia picks at hers, pushing it around on her plate. She's deep in thought, a little furrow between her brows. I let her be. She's been through a lot in the last twenty-four hours. She needs time to think and process. That's always been her way.

When something big happens, she needs time to digest it, think it through, and find out where it fits and how. I love that about her. The way her mind works is fascinating to me. She always has something going on in there. The things she thinks about are as intriguing as the way she thinks. It's never small shit. She thinks about world changing shit. Those deep, philosophical questions and situations that give most people a headache light a fire inside her mind.

I never knew intelligence could be so fucking sexy until I met her.

As often as her gaze drifts toward me, I know I'm one of the things occupying her mind. She doesn't know where she stands with me, or where things stand between us. I don't think I've made it clear enough to settle her mind and give her peace. I need to fix that.

"Come on," I say, holding a hand out to her after I clear our plates.

She blinks as if startled to see me standing beside her. She glances down at my hand and then places hers in it, not asking any of the questions on the tip of her tongue, the ones clouding those pretty eyes.

Mischief lifts his head to look at me and then seems to decide Gia is safe with me. He lays his head back down. I help her down from her stool and then lead her back into the living room and through to my office. Once we're inside, I flip the light on and wait patiently. She gasps as soon as she sees what I wanted her to see.

"Bryant," she whispers, drifting toward the grand piano as if in a dream. During the day, light filters in from the three windows on each side, bathing the area in warmth and sunshine. She runs a hand across the polished ebony and then trails her fingertips across the keys, allowing little notes to spill out into the room. "You don't play the piano."

"I don't."

"Then why?"

"Because you play, Gia baby," I murmur.

"Bryant," she whispers again.

Months before I deployed, she told me she missed playing, but couldn't afford a piano. Her little sister has a lot of medical problems, and she helps her mom take care of the bills. I bought her this piano the very next week. I wanted to give it to her then, but I knew she wouldn't accept it. I had it brought here instead, so she'd always have a place in here with me.

"Why didn't you write me?" she asks, her voice cracking with emotion.

"I did write you," I say, striding across the room toward her. I dip my hand into my pocket and pull out the letter I wrote. The envelope is so tattered it's barely hanging on. The ink on her name and address is virtually gone, rubbed away by the natural oil of my fingertips.

Her gaze drifts from my face to the letter, her expression crumbling when she sees how worn and tattered it is.

"Most guys in the military carry something with them to help remind them what they're fighting for, or to bring them luck," I murmur, coming to a stop directly in front of her, so close I can feel her sweet breath touch my cheek with every exhalation. "A lot of the time, it's something that has value only to them and the people who know them. This is what I carried, Gia. Every day I was over there, I kept this in my pocket. I didn't want to tell you in a letter how I felt about you. I wanted to be standing in front of you, looking into those beautiful eyes."

"H-how do you feel about me?"

"There isn't a word strong enough to describe what I feel for you," I murmur, holding her gaze so she sees the truth in mine. "I know peace and joy because of you. I've found hope and home because of you. I don't merely love you, Gia baby. My heart beats for you. My entire world *is* you. I'm so fucking in love with you, the thought of not having you guts me."

"Bryant," she whispers, a tear spilling down her cheek.

"I've been in love with you since I met you." I reach out and cup her cheek, rubbing away that tear. "I wanted to tell you a thousand times, but I didn't want to ask you to wait for me, Gia. If something had happened to me...I didn't want you to suffer that sort of pain."

"I would have anyway," she whispers.

"I'm starting to get that." I press my forehead to hers. "You're so much fucking stronger than I am. I read every word you sent me. Memorized them. I should have sent the letter. I should have told you how I felt. But I knew if I sent you this letter, your whole world would change. You'd wait for me...and a girl like you can do a helluva lot better than a man like me."

"No, I can't," she chokes, more tears streaming down her face. "There is no one better for me than you, Bryant. Don't you know that? It's been you since the moment I first saw you. Whether you're standing in front of me or fighting in Syria or somewhere else, it will *always* be you."

"Say it," I plead quietly, not above getting on my knees and begging for what I want.

"I love you."

Those three words, whispered so sweetly, wash through me like a healing wind, soothing raw places that nothing else has ever touched, those soul-deep wounds that war left behind, and the older ones. Those that were formed long before I ever looked down the barrel of a rifle. My whole life, I've been on my own. Not anymore. Not ever again.

My lips meet hers, softly sealing the words we just spoke. Hers are so damn soft and warm. Kissing her is like coming home or finding it for the first time ever.

I tug her closer, kiss her deeper. The salt of her tears touches my tongue, and then that taste that I already recognize as her does too. It's sweet and sustaining, breathing life into me.

A whimper ripples from her, pulled from somewhere deep within that beautiful body. Her arms wrap around my neck, her fingers delving into my short hair and scratching at my scalp. My entire body reacts, rising up as if in response to a lightning strike.

The letter slips from my hands. I lose myself in the kiss, our tongues dancing together as it grows deeper, more wild...as ravenous as I've been for her for so fucking long. She kisses me back the same way, as if she can't get close enough or feel me deeply enough.

I feel the piano bench behind my knees, and sit, pulling her down to straddle my lap. She struggles to get her skirt out of the way so she can move, growing frustrated and impatient. I don't even think about it. I just grasp the fabric in my hands and rip it, unwilling to let anything stand in the way of this moment or make it anything less than perfect for her.

She purrs in my arms as if she approves.

For long minutes, we just kiss, learning one another. Like the way she trembles when I stroke her sides, or the sound of her whimper when I bite her lip. Or the way my entire body catches fire when she does the same thing to me. Before long, it's not enough for either of us. After a year and a half, we're both aching, both desperate. I want inside her, want to possess every piece of her and let her possess every piece of me.

I trail my hands down her back to grip that round ass in my hands. She's so fucking soft everywhere. I use my grip to grind her against my erection, letting her feel how badly I want her, how fucking much I need her.

I hurt for her. God, how I hurt.

"Bryant," she cries out, latching onto my shoulders. That sweet voice crying my name is exactly as sexy as I always knew it would be. It sets me ablaze exactly as quickly as I always knew it would.

Everything but her fades to background noise. I trail my lips down her throat and collarbone, tasting every inch of exposed skin I can. She writhes on top of me, searching for a rhythm, for pleasure. I let her experiment, let her play. She's a virgin. Every first she has will be with me. Every last will be too.

Her blouse parts as easily as her skirt did, though with significantly less damage. The buttons are those snap closed ones, easily pulled apart. I strip her out of it, and then bite my tongue hard to keep from coming in my pants like a teenager at the sight of her.

"Jesus Christ, Gia," I breathe, devouring her alive with my eyes. Her bra is sexy black lace with red accents. It looks like pure sin against her ivory skin. Her nipples are hard points jutting up against the fabric. The curve of her waist and the swell of her belly are equally as sexy to me. I love that there's enough of her to grip onto and sink into.

"Bryant!" she sobs when I capture one nipple between my teeth, teasing her until she's writhing all around on my lap, her little panties and my jeans soaked with her juices.

My hands shake as I unclasp the bra. I damn near tear the delicate fabric before it finally gives way. She holds it in place with her hands, slowly letting it go and revealing herself to my hungry gaze. Her tits are incredible. I knew that before I saw them but fuck me. They're round and full, the nipples a pretty pink color that has my cock leaking.

I push them together, massaging them, kissing them everywhere I can reach. I worship them with my mouth and hands, leaving my marks all over them. She cries out again and again, arching back until she's all but bowed over the piano. Her skin flushes, her cries turning more desperate.

We should be in the bedroom for her first time, but I can't seem to make myself let her go long enough to get us there. Instead, I strip her out of her torn skirt, growling like a beast when I see that her panties match the bra. Her bare slit taunts me through the sheer fabric, so fucking tiny and wet.

I pull her away from the piano long enough to close the lid over the keys and then rake her panties down her legs. She cries out in shock when I boost her up onto the piano.

"Let me see you, Gia baby," I demand, yanking my shirt off over my head.

The two unique colors of her eyes have bled together, her pupils dilated with desire. She's trembling for me, her beautiful body shaking. Her tongue touches her bottom lip, sliding along that pretty bow as she sweeps her gaze all over me, looking at me like she wants to eat me alive too.

I love knowing that my body gives her pleasure.

She stops moving, stops breathing when she sees the tattoo along my ribcage. It's her signature, copied from a note she left me one morning.

"I got it before I left," I murmur, running my hands up and down her legs. Her skin feels like silk. I'm already addicted to touching her, to feeling it beneath my palms. "Wanted to have a piece of you with me in case..."

"In case you didn't come home," she whispers.

"No. In case I did, and you weren't mine," I say.

"I would have waited forever." Her eyes meet mine, burning with sincerity. "You're the only man I've ever felt this way about. You're the only one I ever will. I never would have stopped waiting for you."

I lean forward to press a grateful kiss on her thigh. The sweet scent of her arousal hits me. I groan, my dick so hard he's liable to break off if he doesn't get a little relief soon. But I have to taste her first. I have to know if she's as good as I always imagined, if she sounds as sweet as I dreamed. It's a literal requirement at this point. I might actually fucking die if I don't feel her coming on my tongue before she's wrapped around my cock.

"Spread your legs, Gia baby," I say, my voice guttural, dark with need. "Let me see that pretty little thing."

She gives me what I want, slowly, shyly, parting her thighs to reveal her pussy to me. And God, I knew she would completely knock my world out of orbit. I wasn't wrong.

"Jesus, baby," I growl, stunned by how wet she is, by how badly she needs me. My girl is hurting for me, her perfect little cunt swollen, her clit hard. Her pink folds glisten with her juices. They drip down her slit, wetting her thighs and the piano beneath her. She is so goddamn pretty everywhere. I've never seen anything as beautiful as she is right now, sitting atop her piano with her back arched, her tits out, her legs spread, and those gorgeous eyes dazed and dilated.

"Bryant, I need...I need..." She doesn't know what she needs, but I do.

She needs me to lick that little cunt until she creams.

"Hold on," I tell her, moving between her legs, eager to introduce her to all those dirty pleasures she read about, the ones she'll only ever experience with me.

I give her time to grasp the edges of the piano cover, and then I yank her ass to the edge and set to work. I want to take it slow, savor every moment with her, but I can't. Her smell, the sight of her, every single thing about her has me ready to fall on her like a slavering beast.

I bury my tongue in her pussy, licking from her asshole to her clit. She's thick honey, juicy berries, and sweet cream all rolled into one. Her taste blasts through every bit of self-control I have. The bonds snap, sheared in half by the sultry, decadent cry issuing from her lips.

The possessive, demanding part of myself that wants to fuck and claim and own roars to the surface. She's mine. All mine. No one else gets to touch her, kiss her, or fuck her but me. This cunt, that lush, ripe body, every part of her is mine now.

I grip her ass hard, riding her against my tongue...my chin...my lips and nose. I don't lick her pussy. I fucking devour it, unable to stop myself or slow down. I've dreamed about this moment every day for the last year and a half, ached and burned for it.

This cunt is my personal heaven, her body is my playground.

I lick and suck and bite, playing with her clit and tight fuckhole while she pants and shakes and screams. Her juices drip down my chin. I lap them up, not caring if I make a mess of us. I'll wear her with pride, lick this little thing every goddamn day if she'll let me.

"Bryant, Bryant," she chants, rocking her hips. She claws at my shoulders, pulls the short strands of my hair. She's a goddess, taking what I give her and then demanding more. She chants that word too, says it over and over again. *More, more. Please, more.*

I stand up, boosting her up onto the top of the piano to give myself more room to work. She wraps those pale, trembling thighs around my head, arching backward. Her hands scrabble on the polished ebony, searching for something to ground her.

I run my tongue in circles around her clit, try to push the tip of my finger inside her. She's so damn tight. Jesus. I don't think she's even had a vibrator inside her before. I fucking love knowing that.

Her legs start shaking, her cries growing louder.

I seam my lips around her hard little clit, creating suction.

She wails as she shatters apart for me, her legs clamped tight around my head, her body rising and falling like a wave cresting. Another flood of cream soaks my face.

I nearly fucking sob with relief when my finger slips inside her. I quickly add another, stretching her, trying to loosen her up to take me so I don't hurt her when I get my cock in her. It's a helluva lot bigger than my fingers, and she's tight as can be.

She screams my name when I find her g-spot. I roar, triumphant, so fucking turned on I can't breathe through the waves of possessive pride assailing me.

Somehow, I manage to free my cock with my tongue and the fingers of one hand still buried in her cunt, wringing her out. I wrap my fist around myself and squeeze, trying like hell not to come until I'm inside her.

I slip my fingers from her pussy, release her clit. She's still trembling beneath me, mindless, boneless. *Mine.* One heel dangles haphazardly from her foot, knocked askew. The other is already on the floor. Her auburn hair is wild and damp with sweat. Her body is flushed pink, her lips swollen. She looks wrecked, and so damn beautiful my heart aches.

I jerk my pants and boxers down and then gently pry her off the piano. The leather bench is warm beneath my bare ass. I wrap her legs around my waist, pulling her into my lap.

"Fuck," I curse, my stomach clenching when I feel the heat of her pussy against my bare cock. She's burning hot, her folds sticky with her juices and my saliva.

She feels it too and moans. Her body is limp in my arms, her head lolling against my shoulder. Her chest heaves as she sucks air into her lungs like she's starved for oxygen. Little whimpers still escape her lips, rolling over me like music.

"Hold on to me, Gia baby," I murmur, pressing kisses in the sweaty mass of her hair.

She manages to obey my command and wraps her arms around me, clinging. I feel her nails in my shoulder blades. I want them embedded there, lifelong reminders that she's mine and I'm hers and nothing will ever change that now.

We've suffered and hurt and ached for a year and a half, both torn apart, both bleeding for one another. That's over with now. No more waiting. No more hurting. I will never again keep how I feel from her or hurt her. For the rest of my life, I'll protect her as fiercely as I ever defended this country. She's the purpose in my life, the reason I was brought into this world. I feel that truth taking root deep in my bones, sprouting like seeds. I was made to love her and to be loved by her. There isn't a single force in existence stronger than that.

"I don't want anything between us," I tell her, lifting her up to press the head of my cock to her hole. "When I pop your cherry, it'll be with my bare cock."

"Yes," she mumbles, the word thick, garbled. The flood of arousal between her legs is clear enough though. She wants me bare too.

"If I have my way, you'll be pregnant before I pull out of this little thing tonight, Gia." I've thought about that a thousand times too, about watching her grow with my child, watching her shower our children with all the love in her heart.

"Yes," she says again. The word is stronger this time, more lucid.

"Then kiss me, baby, and let me taste heaven."

She tips her head back, seeking my lips. They meet like long parted lovers, exultant, sweet, eager. I wrap my hands around her hips, hating that I have to hurt her to love her. She slides down my cock slowly, letting me in inch by inch. I have to grit my teeth to keep from coming when her heat surrounds the broad head. She feels so fucking good, like her body was made to take mine.

Her distressed whimper cracks my heart in half.

I deepen our kiss, sending up a regretful apology, wishing like hell I could take the pain for her as her cherry pops on my cock. Triumph soars through me, sending my heart into flight with it. She cries out in pain, those nails scoring deep into my skin.

"Breathe, Gia baby," I plead, touching my forehead to hers. Focusing on her when she's wrapped so tightly around my cock is hard, Jesus, is it ever hard. But she comes first in all things, in all ways. Always. "Come on, pretty baby, breathe for me."

"It hurts."

My heart cracks in half again.

"I know, baby. I know." I press adoring kisses to her lips, her cheeks, her eyes. I taste her tears and my soul cries out in protest. "It'll never feel like this again. From now on, my body will only ever give you pleasure, Gia baby. Breathe for me."

She sucks in a deep breath, lets it out in a shaky whimper. Does it again, and then again.

Little by little, the tension ekes from her body. She turns pliant in my arms. Pain turns to passion and then to pleasure. She wriggles in my lap, sliding down my cock another inch.

"Bryant," she whispers, awe in her voice. Her wide eyes meet mine, dazed and so full of emotion I feel it in my soul. "I love you."

I feel that in my soul too, feel the way it sighs for her.

I wrap her hair up in my hand, pull her mouth back down to mine. A moan ripples through the room, though I don't know if it's mine or hers. I'm so lost in her. So lost. Jesus. She's everywhere, eclipsing everything else.

"Move with me, baby," I whisper against her lips, letting her hair go to show her how to move. It doesn't take her long to catch on. Within moments, we're moving together like we've done this a thousand times. She rises and falls on my cock, taking me to the hilt and then rising up to start all over again. My world condenses down to her. To us.

"I love you so much," she cries against my lips. "I can't...I don't..."

"I know," I whisper. "I feel it too, Gia. You're my world, the reason I breathe. God, you feel so fucking good wrapped around me like this. I want to keep you here forever."

"Please." Her hands slip along my back, clutching and releasing as she writhes, searching for what she needs to tip her over the edge, for the things she can't put into words.

I grip her tighter, fuck her harder. Her tits bounce in my face. I wrap my lips around one nipple, adding to her pleasure and to mine. Every part of her gives me so much pleasure. I didn't know it could be like this, so consuming, so perfect.

She bounces in my lap, taking everything I give her and then asking for more, more. Until I'm slamming her down on my dick only to lift her off and drop her again. Over and over until I'm dizzy with the pleasure, wracked by the need to come, and to feel her coming on me.

"Fucking hell," I growl, my balls drawing up when she claws down my back. That lick of pain drives me out of my mind. I fuck her hard, yanking her down on me again and again. She cries out every time, my name a broken crack of sound that serves only to drive me higher, make me harder.

"I'm going to ruin you," I tell her. "Make you live for this and what I do to you, Gia baby. You won't be able to make it through a day without crawling into my lap, onto my cock."

"I a-already won't!" she cries back, her tone caught between offense and joy.

I grip her ass cheeks in my hands, spreading them apart, grinding her against the root of my cock. Her surprised shout sends another bolt of triumph lancing through me. I do it again, bouncing her and then grinding against her clit.

"I need you to come, Gia," I say, biting my tongue, trying like hell to hold off my own orgasm. I can already feel it clawing its way to the surface, more powerful than anything I've ever felt before. Everything is new with her, everything is fucking perfect because of her.

"Bryant, I...I..." she trails off, letting out a frustrated whine.

"You need more, baby?" I bounce her against me again, playing with her asshole. One day, I'll get in there too, own that part of her too. She bounces against my thighs, landing with a loud clap of sound each time. Her pussy gets wetter, soaking me, her juices dripping down my balls.

I bring my hand down on her ass in a hard spank.

"Come. Now," I growl, biting her lip at the same time.

The sound of her screaming my name as she breaks for me will stay with me for the rest of my life. It's so goddamn sexy. Fucking Christ. I've been in her once and I'm already addicted, already craving more.

She claws down my back again, sobbing and writhing as her pussy locks down on me so tightly I cry out, stunned. She milks the come out of me, demanding my release.

I give it to her, pounding into her until the cord snaps.

"Gia!" I roar as I come, my entire body rigid, gripped by pleasure so intense it blinds me, stealing the air from my lungs. Spurt after spurt shoots up my shaft, pumping into her. It's so good it hurts. Jesus. It hurts so fucking good. I groan, seeking her lips.

Our kiss is sloppy, joyous as we come together in a rush of sticky juices and slavish devotion, finally whole, finally together.

Chapter Six

Gia

"HOW ARE YOU FEELING, Gia baby?" Bryant asks, pulling me closer to him in his big bed. He carried me up here not long ago. He's wrapped so tightly around me I feel him everywhere. His lips brush my shoulder, his right hand sliding down my lower stomach to send quivers of excitement through me. His fingertips brush my mound before stilling. "You sore?"

"No. I'm perfect," I whisper, melting into him.

He hums quietly, kissing my shoulder again. "Sex makes you quiet," he observes.

A smile curves my lips. "Yeah? I think it makes you talkative."

"I spent a year without saying anything to you," he says, far more seriously than my teasing comment warranted.

"I hurt you by keeping shit to myself. I'm not doing that anymore. I'm going to talk your fucking ear off. Tell you a thousand times a day how much I love you."

"Okay," I say, my smile overtaking my face. His deep voice is my favorite sound in the world. I love the way it rumbles from his lips and vibrates against my back. I love when he growls and gets grumpy and mutters and curses. I missed hearing him so much while he was overseas.

"You've always been more than I deserve, you know that?" His lips touch my shoulder again.

"And you've always been the only thing I wanted."

His hand climbs back toward my belly. "I hope I got you pregnant," he says, splaying his fingers wide. His big hand nearly spans the width of my abdomen, his pinky and thumb not far from touching each of my hips. "Think I dreamed about that every fucking night."

"Me too," I whisper, tears stinging my eyes at the thought of having his babies. I've always wanted kids. My brother and sister are younger than I am. Helping my mom care for them when I was growing up was one of my favorite things.

My little sister still comes and spends weekends with me sometimes to give my mom a break. I love having her here. She's been through a lot, but she's the sweetest girl. She's fourteen, but she's so smart. So is Dante. We're all close. I hope he chooses Vanderbilt so he's still close by.

I've had enough of missing the people I love to last me a lifetime.

"Can I ask you a question?" I ask Bryant, playing with his fingers. They're so much bigger than mine. He makes me feel so small and delicate. I've never had that before and I love how it feels.

"Anything," he promises.

"Your letter..." I hesitate, not sure what I want to ask or how to go about it.

"You want to know what it says?"

"Yes, but that's not my question. You said you carried it the whole time. Does that mean you wrote it before you left?"

He's quiet for a minute. "I did. I intended to send it to you the day I shipped out. But the thought of asking you to wait for me..." he sighs, ruffling strands of my hair. "It's a hell of a thing to ask of anyone, Gia baby. Especially when you don't know if you'll be coming home. I couldn't ask you to take that risk for me and live with myself."

I don't think I'll ever really understand how that feels but I hear the distress in his voice, the regret. I don't want that between us anymore. We're together and we're happy and none of the other stuff matters anymore. I could spend the rest of my life being angry about it. He could spend the rest of his regretting it. It would just hurt us both. I don't want him to spend the rest of his life regretting the way things happened. I don't want to spend mine angry.

I think we've had enough of that already. Now, all I want is to love him and be loved by him. To fall asleep to him and wake up to him. To laugh with him again and be with him. The other stuff doesn't matter.

"I forgive you," I whisper, shifting around until I'm able to roll over to look at him. I place my hand against his cheek, looking into those green eyes. "I don't want it between us anymore."

"Me either," he murmurs, tipping his head forward to brush his lips across my forehead. "I don't want anything between me and that body except the clothes you wear around other men."

"Caveman," I mutter, rolling my eyes and smiling. He's crazy.

"Yeah, I am," he says, not denying it. "When it comes to you, I'm possessive and jealous and greedy as hell, Gia baby. The fact that other men exist around you pisses me off. You're mine and I won't ever share any part of you."

"How do you think I feel? Women at work are always staring at you."

"Are they?" He blinks at me, seeming surprised. "I never noticed."

I shake my head, laughing because I know he's telling me the truth. I never really thought about it before, but he never looked at anyone else. When we were together, he was always too busy looking at me. It was the same way for me. All I've ever been able to see is him. He's the only man I *want* to see.

He catches my hand in his. His lips turn down into a frown. "You need to marry me."

I freeze.

"Don't like you not already having my name."

"Are you...asking me to marry you?" I whisper.

"No."

My heart quivers, threatening to break in half.

"I'm not asking, Gia baby," he growls, pulling me closer when I try to break away from him. "There is no question involved. You're mine. I'm yours. We're getting married, preferably sooner rather than later. I know you'll want your family there, so I'll give you a little time to plan it. But you will be marrying me before our baby gets here."

"It takes the average couple up to a year to conceive," I mumble, the first thing that comes to mind. He wants to marry me. Holy crap.

He quirks a brow at me and smirks, all cocky and bossy and hot. "If I didn't get you pregnant this first time, I will the next, you better believe that. You're not leaving this house until you're carrying my kid."

"Yes."

It's his turn to freeze.

I crawl on top of him, forcing him to flip over onto his back. His erection nestles against my center, hard and insistent. His eyes meet mine, so full of love, I can't catch my breath. It's lodged somewhere in my throat alongside my heart.

"Yes," I say again, placing my hands on his chest to keep me balanced. "I'll marry you, Bryant. Any damn day of the week, I'll marry you."

"Yeah?" he whispers, his voice a choked wisp of sound.

"Yes."

I scream when he sits up, flipping me onto my back in one easy move. Before my head hits the bed, he's got his hand behind it. He comes down over me, blocking out everything but him again. His lips meet mine, his kiss ravenous, scorching hot. I wrap my legs around his waist, getting lost in him and the way he tastes, like fine wine and sweet berries and home. I could kiss this man forever and never want for anything else.

Somehow, he ends up inside me again. Somehow, he takes me even higher than the first time, loving me so sweetly that I sob his name as I fall apart for him all over again. He falls with me, whispering my name into my throat as if it's a prayer or a song, full of reverence and devotion.

"Missed you so damn much," I mumble, sprawled across his chest as his hands drift through my hair, gently un-tangling it. His heart plays a steady rhythm beneath my ear, lulling me to the edge of sleep. I'm safe and warm and so damn happy. I feel like I'm floating somewhere near heaven, too full of little bubbles of bliss to come back down to earth.

"Every day," he whispers into my hair. "Sleep, Gia baby, and dream of me."

"Always," I try to say, but the only sound I make is a little sigh. And then I'm out.

Mischief barking yanks me out of sleep what feels like only moments later. I sit up, disoriented. It's completely dark, the only light coming from the skylight over the bed. The moon isn't in the same position it was, alerting me to the fact that I've been sleeping far longer than a few minutes.

"Bryant?" I whisper, feeling across the bed for him.

"I'm right here," he says from somewhere across the room.

"What's going on? Where's Mischief?"

"I don't know, but I'm going to find out," Bryant murmurs, his voice hard, tense.

Something is wrong. Hairs all over my body stand up, fear whispering through me. I grab the comforter, dragging it up over me like that's going to help. It isn't, but I'm naked and scared and I think someone might be in the house.

I see a thick shadow moving toward me and cry out.

"Shh, Gia baby," Bryant whispers.

A wave of relief hits me so hard I think my heart stops for a second.

"Take this," Bryant says, reaching out for my hand. A second later, he drops a gun into it.

"Bryant."

"Take it, Gia," he growls.

My fingers close around the weapon, my heart kicking into high gear. He taught me to shoot before he left, told me that I should know how to defend myself. I never thought I'd see the day where I might actually have to do it, though. I'm not sure if I *can* actually do it.

"Don't leave this room unless you hear my voice," he says and then I feel his hand in my hair, pulling my head back. His lips meet mine in a hard kiss. "I love you, Gia."

"Bryant," I whimper, tears rolling down my cheeks.

"Mischief, *ke mne*!" he says, pulling away. He whistles one sharp note.

Mischief comes barreling into the room a moment later, his paws skidding as he goes from the rug to the hardwood. He seems to know exactly where everything is at though because a few seconds later, I feel his tail smacking the bed.

"*Pozor*," Bryant says to him.

Mischief instantly goes into work mode, growling savagely. I hear him pacing back and forth beside the bed, standing between me and anything that might come through the door.

"I love you," Bryant says again, and then he's gone, slipping back into the shadows and out into the hall. He takes my heart with him.

"Please," I pray, willing to plead to whatever god will listen. "Please keep him safe."

Part of me wants to fall apart, but I can't do that. Bryant's out there alone and someone might be in the house. There's no time for me to break. I have to think.

My phone.

I need my phone.

"Shit," I mutter, my heart sinking. My phone is still in my bag, which is in the living room. Bryant's phone is out there too. He tossed it on the table as soon as we were through the front door. Which means I'm screwed. I can't call for help or do anything but sit and wait and pray.

Tears drip down my face. My heart races. I don't let myself panic though. I can't. What if someone is out there and they get past Bryant? I have to be calm.

Mischief growls as he paces, waiting just like me. Only he's probably been in a situation like this before. I haven't. The dog is better prepared to handle this than I am.

If something happens to Bryant, I'll never forgive him. He can't make me his and then leave me alone. I've had him for all of a handful of hours, and I already know losing him would destroy me. He's always been the only thing I need, the one person that I'd give up anything to keep. I love him beyond all reason.

"Please keep him safe," I plead.

Time seems to drag on forever. I strain to hear anything, any little hint of what's happening out there. There's nothing though. All I hear is my own heart beating and Mischief.

I set the gun beside me and tug on the sheet, wrapping it around me like a toga. Mr. Laughlin already saw my panties. He doesn't get to see my boobs too.

If he does something to hurt Bryant, I'll spend every day of my life making sure he pays in the most painful ways possible.

"Gia."

"Bryant!" I drop the gun back to the bed again and leap up, racing across the room to him. I hit him like a shockwave, knocking him back a step.

"Jesus, baby," he growls, boosting me up into his arms. He wraps them around me, holding me tight.

"You're safe," I sob, running my hands all over him, checking for injuries.

"I'm okay. Everything is okay," he says, his voice soft. "Mischief, *volno*."

Mischief immediately stops growling.

"What happened?" I ask, clinging to Bryant as he carries me across the room. "Who was out there? Why was Mischief going crazy?"

"It's Grant."

"Grant? Grant broke into your house?"

"No. What the fuck? Of course not." He tries to pry me off him to put me back in the bed, but I refuse to let go. "Baby, you gotta let me go so we can get dressed."

I reluctantly loosen my grip, allowing him to sit me on the edge of the bed.

A second later, the bedside lamp clicks on, flooding the room with light. I blink my eyes, trying to adjust, and then look at Bryant. He's dressed in a pair of sweats, a gun tucked into his waistband. He has claw marks down his arms and back.

My cheeks heat at the thought of my boss seeing him like this. He probably knows we had sex which is super awkward.

"You gotta get dressed, Gia baby," Bryant says, picking up the handgun from the bed. He pulls his out of his pocket and carries them both over to the closet. He disappears inside for a moment, putting them back into the gun safe he keeps in there.

I hop up and look around for my clothes, but they're still strewn all over the floor in his office. I spot one of his t-shirts thrown over the back of the chair in the corner, so I grab that and put it on. Despite my size, the shirt hits me at mid-thigh.

Bryant steps out of the closet, pulling a t-shirt on over his head. His eyes come to me and soften. "You look good in my clothes, Gia," he mutters.

"My bag is still downstairs," I remind him.

"Shit."

"Why do we have to get dressed? What's going on?" I demand.

"Mr. Laughlin was located about an hour ago."

"What? Seriously?" I gape at him, shocked.

Bryant's jaw tics. "He was trying to break into your house through a bedroom window," he says, striding across the room toward me. He stops directly in front of me, crooking my chin up until our eyes meet. "He fled when they spotted him, and then tried to run down an officer, Gia baby. They shot him."

"Oh my gosh," I whisper. "Is he...? Did they...?"

Bryant dips his head in a tiny nod. His gaze flits across my face, full of worry. "I don't want you thinking this was your fault in any way," he says, pulling me into his arms. "He made his own choices, and those don't have anything to do with you, all right?"

I bob my head in a nod, too shocked to form words. Never in a million years did I imagine that Mr. Laughlin was this dangerous. He was a jerk, true enough. But he didn't strike me as someone prone to violence or someone willing to throw everything away just to make a quick buck. I feel sorry for him and the people who cared about him. And relieved for me, that I wasn't at home when it happened.

I'm safe because Bryant kept me that way. He understood the danger I was in better than I did, and he made sure I would be safe. Even when he thought I hated him, he protected me. He's always protected me the same way. Standing in his arms, I know he always will.

"I love you," I whisper to him, humbled that someone like him, so brave and powerful and *good* chose someone like me. He thinks he doesn't deserve me, but he's wrong. I don't deserve him. But he's mine anyway. I'm keeping him anyway.

"I love you too, Gia baby," he whispers.

Chapter Seven
Bryant

"TELL HER TO TAKE the rest of the week off," Grant mutters to me as I follow him out to his truck. It's already almost four in the morning. The police just left. Gia's inside with Mischief watching over her. He hasn't left her side since Grant showed up three hours ago.

I wasn't sure what the fuck was going on when Mischief started barking. All I could think was that Laughlin had found Gia. I was fully prepared to put a bullet in him. Instead, I found out that Chattanooga P.D. took care of the problem for me. He won't ever bother Gia again.

Gia seems to be handling the news well. She's been quiet though.

"Plan on it," I tell Grant as he pops the locks to climb into his truck.

"You two worked out your shit?" he asks me.

I jerk my chin in a nod.

"Good," he says, grinning at me. "Come see me when she's ready to come back. I have a proposition for you. A job."

"At D.I.?"

"Tremaine and Associates," he says, referring to the law firm he helps manage for his wife. It belonged to her grandmother before she passed. "Regan needs some muscle to keep a witness safe. Seems like it's right up your alley."

"I'll come see you."

"Take care of her," he orders me and then climbs into the truck.

I watch until he hits the end of the driveway and then I head back inside. He doesn't need to tell me to take care of my girl. There's nothing I want to do more than take care of her every need, hold her, spoil her, love her like she deserves.

"Gia baby?" I stop in shock when I cross the threshold to find her sitting on the couch, sobbing. It takes me half a second to process that she isn't crying over Laughlin's death. She's got my letter in her hands.

Mischief shoots me a reproachful look and then grunts and moves out of the way. I'm at Gia's side in a second, sweeping her up into my arms to hold her.

"Baby," I whisper, my heart breaking. I fucking hate it when she cries.

"I'm s-s-sorry," she sobs.

I rub her back, trying to soothe her. My eyes drift to the letter still in her hands. I gently pry it free and set it on the arm of the couch.

"It's so b-beautiful."

"You read it?"

"Y-yes."

"Every word of it is as true now as it was the day I wrote it, Gia baby," I rasp, pressing my lips to her temple. "Every word."

"Bryant!" she sobs.

I smile, knowing she's not mad about it even if she sounds mad. She's overwhelmed.

It's been a helluva few days for her.

But the thing about Gia, the thing that even she forgets sometimes, is that she's stronger than anyone I've ever met before. Even when she's hurting, even when she's sad, she's fiercely gentle, capable of anything. She's all the good shit in the world—the kindness and compassion, the intelligence and ambition.

People love to ask soldiers why they fight. Our answer—not the one we give people but the one we keep deep in our hearts—is the same every time. We fight for people like Gia. Those who shouldn't ever have to know the horrors some men are capable of committing. Those who make home so much more than just a place to rest our heads. Those who make all the nightmares and the demons and the horrors worth it.

We fight for love, because at the end of the day, it's the only thing that matters.

"I love you," I murmur, running my hands through her silky hair. There's so much of it, but it's so damn soft, just like the rest of her. It smells like her too, like blackberries and jasmine and peace. I missed her smell as much as anything else.

Eventually, she stops crying and falls silent in my arms. I lift her up and carry her back to bed. She's awake when I lay her on the bed, her eyes red and puffy but focused on me. Even with her face ravaged by tears, she's beautiful. My cock stirs, as enamored of her as ever.

"I don't want to leave here," she whispers as I strip her clothes from her body and then yank my shirt off over my head.

I drop my shirt and meet her gaze. "You aren't going anywhere but to sleep, Gia baby."

"That's not what I mean," she says, rolling her eyes at me. Her lips lift into a little smile though, which makes my dick even harder. Swear to God, if I could keep her in this bed, wearing nothing but a smile, I'd die the happiest man to ever live.

"You asking to move in with me, Gia?"

"Maybe," she whispers, all shy and sweet. Her cheeks heat, her eyes shifting away from me. "I just...thinking about him in my house gave me the creeps before everything else. Now, the thought of going back there makes my stomach hurt."

I yank my sweats off and toss them aside before crawling into the bed beside her. I hit the light and the pull her warm, naked body up against me. She snuggles in like a little kitten getting comfortable, practically purring.

I smile in the dark, happy as hell I'm not going to have to convince her to move in with me. As far as I'm concerned, that shit was settled before I followed her home today. It was definitely settled when I saw that Laughlin had broken in. And, if there was any hint of a question left about her moving in after that, falling asleep with her in my arms settled it permanently.

"Is that the only reason you want to move in?" I ask, running my hand down her back to grab her ass. I'll definitely be sleeping with it in my hands for the foreseeable future. Being able to touch her however and whenever I want is addicting.

"No," she says, that sultry quality to her voice that turns me on like nothing else. The one that tells me she's thinking about me and her dirty books again. "I love your house. And Mischief."

"Is that all?"

"I love your kitchen?"

I growl and roll over, pinning her beneath me. She squeals with laughter.

"What else?" I demand, hovering over her. My dick settles between her legs, which makes her moan. As much as I want to fuck her again, I know I can't. She'll be too sore to walk tomorrow if I get inside her again tonight.

But that doesn't mean I can't get her off real quick.

"I love this bed," she moans as I wrap her leg around my hip and grind my dick against her clit. She's already soaked, allowing my cock to slide with ease through her folds. My eyes threaten to roll back in my head at how good it feels.

"Gia," I growl, jealous and impatient. I nip at her collarbone before wrapping my lips around her nipple. The hard little bud tastes like heaven.

She arches upward, her back bowing off the bed.

"Tell me," I demand, grinding against her clit over and over until she's squirming beneath me and moaning my name. Her hands run up and down my back before she grabs my ass, trying to pull me closer as her orgasm starts to crash over her. "Tell me, Gia."

"I love you!" she cries, coming all over me.

"Fuck yes," I growl, humping her like a fucking dog in heat. I take her mouth in a hard kiss, possessing her again. It doesn't take long before I'm coming too, covering that little cunt in sticky ropes of my come. Even then, I keep moving, covering us in our juices as we kiss and pant and moan.

"I want to move in with you because I can't imagine sleeping in my bed alone anymore," she whispers when I finally roll us over, pulling her halfway on top of me. She snuggles against my chest, her legs between mine. "We've spent enough time apart."

"We'll go get your shit tomorrow," I promise, kissing her temple.

"Stuff," she corrects me.

I smile in the dark, happier than I've ever been. Complete in a way I've never been.

This girl...Jesus, this girl.

I can't fucking wait to spend the rest of my life protecting her.

Bryant's Letter

G IA BABY,

The plane hasn't even left the tarmac yet, and I'm already missing you like crazy. I've tried a million times to find a way to put into words what you mean to me, but nothing ever seems good enough. Since the day I met you, you've held my heart in the palm of your perfect little hand.

Knowing I have to spend the next 365 days without you is killing me.

365 days without looking into those gorgeous eyes.

365 days without seeing that beautiful smile.

365 days without your laughter.

365 days without your sweet voice.

365 days without you.

I'll be in hell every minute.

I love you. I've loved you since the minute I met you. I should have told you before I left but I knew I couldn't say the words and then walk away from you. I wouldn't have survived it.

It kills me a little to think of you missing me the same way I already miss you. If I could carry that pain for the both of us, I would in an instant. Anything to keep you smiling. But I can't lie to you. Part of me is bastard enough to hope you do miss me. Part of me desperately wants you to never look at anyone else the way you look at me or share with anyone else the things you share with me.

I'm weak when it comes to you, pretty baby. I always have been. I suspect I always will be.

I have no right to ask, but I am anyway. Wait for me, Gia.

I swear, I'm coming home to you.

I love you.

Always Yours,

Bryant

Epilogue

Gia

SIX YEARS LATER

"It looks like I have everything I need from you," I say, glancing from the file in front of me to the man seated on the other side of my desk. Jax Archer is a crazy hot, super sweet billionaire. He's not my type, which seems to start and end at Bryant, but I can appreciate a hunk when I see one.

Jax fits the bill. He's tall and broad, with crewcut brown hair and a wicked jawline. His brown eyes glitter behind his glasses. The glasses give him a hot nerd vibe. But there's no mistaking the lethality in his gaze. Like Bryant, Jax is capable of killing to protect what's his. Which is probably why they get along so well.

It's been six years since Bryant told me how he felt about me. Not much has changed in that time. I'm still hopelessly, wildly in love with him. He's still sexy as hell and as possessive as ever.

A lot of women would probably find that trait problematic, but not me. I love how he is with me, and I know he's the way he is because of everything we went through. For a year and a half, he thought he had to love me from afar. While he was fighting a war, he worried every day that I'd find someone else, marry someone else.

I don't mind that he's a little crazy. I'm a little crazy too. It annoys me to no end when we go out and women try to flirt with him. It pisses him off too. It's so rude that they flirt with him while I'm right there! He gets rude with them when they do it, but it never seems to stop them.

He's mine though, and I don't share.

I love him so much. I'd fight any battle to keep him. Luckily for me, the only battles we fight these days are when we're trying to get our babies down for the night.

They do not go down easy.

Callie, our oldest, is five...going on eighteen. She's far too smart for her own good. If we don't watch her carefully, she's liable to hide under the covers reading all night. Books are magic to her. Since she started learning to read, she never wants to stop. Her library card gets a workout. She's also really fascinated by science. She talks her daddy into doing all sorts of experiments with her.

Our boys, Caleb and Creed, are two and three. They haven't mastered reading yet, but they have mastered video games and sneaking out of bed. They're as bossy as their daddy is. They're both a handful but I love them so much.

I can't wait until Chloe gets here in a few months. I already know she's going to be as incredible as her siblings. I'm so ready to meet her and hold her in my arms. Being pregnant is exhausting, but I love every minute of it. There's something so peaceful about carrying our baby.

Lord knows, Bryant likes when I'm carrying his babies. He can't keep his hands off me when I'm pregnant. Okay, so he can't ever seem to keep his hands off me but when I'm pregnant, he's insatiable. I'm not complaining. What woman wouldn't want her husband to worship her body even when she can't see her own feet?

Nothing has ever made me feel as beautiful or as good as Bryant does when I'm pregnant. He's in me almost every night, and then again in the morning. At least once or twice a week, he pulls me into the bathroom or the pantry to fuck me while the kids watch cartoons.

God, how I love him and the incredible life we have together. He's the sun and moon, and our babies are the stars in my life. They light up my entire universe in a million crazy, amazing ways. All the things Bryant and I went through, all the heartache and sadness...they were worth it.

"We're good here?" Jax asks, glancing at the Rolex on his wrist.

"Yep," I say, smiling. "I'll go through all of the financial data you brought me and draft up an investment plan. We'll go over it next time you come in."

He grins, flashing me his dimples. "You're a lifesaver, Gia." He rises to his feet. "Thank you for taking me on like this."

"No problem." I set his file aside and pull myself to my feet. It's a lot of work with a belly as big as mine. I think Chloe plans to be a linebacker at the rate she's growing. We still have almost three months to go, but I already have trouble seeing my feet.

Jax drops his gaze to my belly and his eyes widen. I think kids freak him out a little. He's in his early thirties and just inherited a massive fortune from his estranged father. Until six months ago, he was a SEAL like Bryant. Now women are coming out of the woodworks to throw themselves at him.

"I was going to offer to bring coffee next time we meet, but I don't think you're allowed to have it with...that," he says.

"You know the word *baby* isn't a curse, right?" I laugh, unable to resist teasing him. He's a great guy, very sweet when he wants to be. Bryant convinced him to come and see me, which is saying something because Bryant doesn't like any of my male clients. Not even the ones old enough to be my great grandfather. He thinks they all want to steal me from him, which is ridiculous.

"Says you," Jax mutters and then his phone dings. He pulls it from his pocket and scowls at it. "I'll see you later, sweetheart. I gotta run."

"See ya."

He ducks out of my office, still glaring at his phone. I don't think he's thrilled about his new life or all the stuff that came with it. Had his father's employees not been counting on him, I'm not so sure he would have accepted the inheritance. But he's a good guy. Letting his dad's empire crumble when it would have cost innocent people their livelihoods wasn't an option.

A few seconds after he leaves, I hear the deep rumble of Bryant's voice and smile. He's just in time to take me to lunch...or maybe to have me for lunch. The thought of the latter sends little fingers of desire twisting through me.

The first time we had sex in my office, I was worried we'd get caught and Grant would have to fire both of us. And then Holly spilled the beans about all the sexcapades her and Ian have gotten up to in her office, which led to Lily confessing about her and Grant having sex in their office. I did the math after that. Grant can't afford to fire us all.

Well, I mean, he can. He's a freaking billionaire. But he won't. At least that's what Lily says. And Grant always does what Lily wants. He's smart like that. I think she could ask him to walk on water and he'd find a way to make it happen.

"Gia baby." Bryant stops in the doorway to my office. His green eyes rove over me, eating me alive. When we're apart for any length of time, he always looks at me the same way, like he's been dying in the desert and I'm an oasis.

I stare at him just as hard. My man is sexy as hell in his black suit and green tie. He's grown his hair out a little over the last couple of years...mostly because I think he likes when I have my hands in it while he's fucking me. That cowlick still fascinates me.

His body is still ridiculously ripped.

Sometimes, I go to the gym with him just to watch him work out. Watching him is fascinating to me. He's a machine, putting all those muscles through their paces. And I shamelessly reap the benefits of all the hard work he puts in.

I'm still thick and curvy, which is just the way Bryant likes me. After I had Callie, I tried to go on a diet to lose the few pounds that refused to disappear. When I told Bryant, he spanked me, fucked me, and then made me promise not to try to change my body to please anyone. He said he loves my body exactly the way it is, and that those few extra pounds only made him want me more.

Needless to say, I gave up on dieting after that.

"Damn, you look good," he growls, pushing the door to my office closed and then turning the lock.

I almost break out in a dance when he prowls toward me, purpose in his eyes and his steps. Looks like I'm getting orgasms for lunch today. Yay me!

"Come here."

I take the hand he holds out to me, allowing him to pull me close. He wraps one arm around me and splays the other across my belly. His lips touch the side of my throat and then he sighs like he always does when we spend any time apart. The sound is colored with relief and tinged with sweetness. I love it so much.

"How are my babies?" he asks.

"We're good," I promise. "Just working on some things for Jax. How's your day?"

"Good. May have a new asset to babysit next week," he murmurs, cuddling me close. Not long after everything happened with Mr. Laughlin, Grant put Bryant in charge of security at the law firm Lily's grandma owned before her death. My man babysits witnesses and anxious experts waiting to testify in high profile cases. It's crazy how corrupt some people are, or how far they'll go to hide their crimes.

I never have to worry about Bryant too much though. He promised me six years ago that he would never leave my side again. I know he'd crawl through every level of hell to keep that promise and make it home safely to me and our babies if he had to do it. We're his world as much as he is ours. He'd do anything for us.

He inches his hand from my belly up to my chest, his fingers closing over my right breast.

"You hungry, Gia baby?" he asks, pinching my nipple.

"No," I moan, tilting my head back to rest it against his chest.

He chuckles, sliding his other hand down my body. His quick fingers make easy work of the button on my skirt, allowing him to slip his hand inside. As soon as I feel his fingers against my center, I whimper.

"You've been thinking about me," he says, humming his approval when he finds how wet I am. My panties are easily flicked to the side. His fingers part my slit, and then his thumb is on my clit.

I writhe against him, biting my lip to keep myself quiet. I've had so much practice at it over the years, but it's still so hard not to cry out for him when he's playing my body like it belongs to him. He knows exactly how and where to touch me to make me burn.

He uses that power now, toying with me until I'm whimpering and clawing at his arm, pleading for release. He doesn't give it to me. Instead, he drags my skirt up my legs and then places a hand on my back, gently pushing until I lean down over the desk.

"Bryant," I whimper when I hear him release his zipper.

He yanks my panties down to my knees, running his hand all over my bare ass. He squeezes my cheeks, separates them, touches the tip of his finger to my back entrance. I squirm beneath him, fighting to stay quiet so we don't get caught.

"Fuck," he growls when he thrusts into me, sinking deep. "I love this little cunt. It's always so fucking wet and ready for me, Gia baby." He wraps a hand around my right hip, holding me still as he pounds into me.

I writhe, clawing at the desk, biting my tongue. It doesn't stop the whimpers and moans I can't ever seem to hold back when he's inside me.

He slips his free hand around me and plays with my clit while he fucks me. Within seconds, I'm racing toward an orgasm.

"Let me feel it," he growls, nipping at my neck. "Been thinking about this pussy all fucking morning, Gia. Give me what I want."

"Bryant," I cry out as the first waves hit me, throwing me headfirst into a rolling orgasm. My knees threaten to buckle as it flings me skyward and sends my world into twirling orbit. Lights flash and dance behind my eyes and my heart races.

"That's it," Bryant growls, his grip on my hip tightening. He thrusts twice more and then grunts. I feel his seed warming my belly and dripping down my inner thigh. He fucks me through it, not stopping until we're both completely wrung out and gasping for breath.

"So beautiful," he whispers, gently sweeping my hair aside to kiss the back of my neck. "Jesus, baby. Just when I think you can't possibly get any hotter, you do." He pulls out of me, groaning, and then grabs tissues to clean me up.

I stay where I'm at, slumped over the desk, as he cleans me up and then fixes my clothes. Once we're both decent again, he sweeps me up in his arms and sits in my chair, cuddling me. I press my face to his throat, kissing him there.

"You sleepy?" he asks, brushing his lips in lazy passes across my forehead.

"Mmhmm," I hum, making him chuckle.

We cuddle for several moments, both blissed out and happy. I love when he's all sweet and cuddly like this. I think my favorite place to be is in his arms after he makes love to me. He's always touching me, kissing me, whispering sweet words into my ear. He makes me feel like the only woman in the world.

"You know what today is?" he asks a moment later, playing with my wedding ring.

"Thursday," I mumble.

"Eight years ago today, we met," he says, his voice soft.

I sit up so I can look at him. His expression is as soft as his voice, his green eyes overflowing with tenderness and adoration. I place my hand on his cheek, feeling his stubble beneath my palm.

"You remember the exact day we met?" I ask.

"Of course I do," he says as if it's the most natural thing in the world. His gaze holds mine captive. "It's the day I realized God actually exists."

"Bryant," I whisper, melting for him.

"It's true, Gia baby," he murmurs, turning his head to kiss my palm. "Until the day I met you, I always assumed He was out there somewhere, but I was never sure. Seeing the shit I saw, doing the shit I did, it's hard not to doubt. But then I saw you for the first time and I knew for sure. There's no fucking way the other half of my soul just randomly showed up in front of me, looking so goddamn beautiful and sweet. It had to be God that brought you to me."

"Bryant," I whisper again, tears stinging at my eyes before slipping down my cheeks.

"I'm not a religious man, baby, but I said a prayer that day." His lips curve into a smile so full of sweetness, I feel it in my soul. "Been saying them every day since, Gia. You're the answer to every single one of them."

"Stop making me cry!" I cry, faceplanting into his chest.

His chuckle rumbles from his big body. He rubs a hand down my back. "I'm not trying to make you cry, Gia baby. I just wanted you to know how fucking much I love you. My life was shit before you waltzed into it. Now, I'm the luckiest motherfucker on the planet. I have you and our kids. A man can't ask for much more than that."

"I'm lucky too," I whisper, wiping my face on his shirt. He chuckles and shakes his head but doesn't say anything about it. He always lets me mess up his clothes when I cry and never complains about it. "You and our babies are the best thing that ever happened to me."

"Yeah?" he asks, smiling at me. It reflects in his eyes, happiness shining like a beacon from those emerald depths.

"Yeah," I whisper. "Had you let me push you away back when you first got home, I think I would have regretted it for the rest of my life. I would have missed you for the rest of my life. I love you, Bryant. More and more every damn day."

His lips meet mine in a sweet kiss, one full of peace and promise.

"I love you too, Gia baby. Always," he says against my lips.

"Always," I whisper back.

Author's Note

I F YOU ENJOYED *PROTECT You*, please consider leaving a review. Reviews are really important for authors like me.

The Love on the Clock series bundle (and bonus scenes) is available in ebook and paperback format!

Get ready to fall in love with the Thorne siblings in the Claimed series! These bossy billionaires and their younger sisters find love in unexpected places in this series of steamy contemporary romances. The first book, Possessing Liberty, is out now!

Possessing Liberty

Falling in love never hurt so good.

Killian

I'm a military man...rough, demanding, and used to being obeyed.

I don't do love. I don't date. I don't have time for either.

But Liberty Connor has me rethinking everything.

One kiss from those sweet lips, and I'm hers.

How do you convince an angel to fall for the devil?

You possess her.

Liberty

Killian Thorne is my worst nightmare.

Bossy, scarred...and hot as Hades.

He offered me a fortune to help him save vulnerable soldiers.

There's just one problem.

Who's going to save me from him when I fall hard for him and his rough ways?

POSSESSING LIBERTY IS OUT NOW.

Follow Nichole

Like free books? Me too! Sign-up for my mailing list at http://authornicholerose.com/newsletter to stay up-to-date on all new releases and for exclusive giveaways and freebies!

Want to connect with me and other readers? Join Nichole Rose's Book Beauties on Facebook!

facebook.com/AuthorNicholeRose/

instagram.com/AuthorNicholeRose

twitter.com/AuthNicholeRose

bookbub.com/authors/nichole-rose

tiktok.com/@authornicholerose

Nichole's Book Beauties

Want to connect with Nichole and other readers? We're building a girl gang! Join Nichole Rose's Book Beauties on Facebook for fun, games, and behind-the-scenes exclusives!

The Instalove Book Club is now in session!

Get the inside scoop from your favorite instalove authors, meet new authors to love, and snag a free book and bonus content from featured authors every month. The Instalove Book Club newsletter goes out once per week!

Join the Club: http://instalovebookclub.com

Also by Nichole Rose

<u>Her Alpha Series</u>

Her Alpha Daddy Next Door

Her Alpha Boss Undercover

Her Alpha's Secret Baby

Her Alpha Protector

Her Date with an Alpha

Her Alpha: The Complete Series

<u>Her Bride Series</u>

His Future Bride

His Stolen Bride

His Secret Bride

His Curvy Bride

His Captive Bride

His Blushing Bride

His Bride: The Complete Series

<u>Claimed Series</u>

Possessing Liberty

Teaching Rowan

Claiming Caroline

Kissing Kennedy

Claimed: The Complete Series

<u>Love on the Clock Series</u>

Adore You

Hold You

Keep You

Protect You

Love on the Clock: The Complete Series

<u>The Billionaires' Club</u>

The Billionaire's Big Bold Weakness

The Billionaire's Big Bold Wish

The Billionaire's Big Bold Woman

The Billionaire's Big Bold Wonder

The Billionaires' Club: The Complete Series

<u>Playing for Keeps</u>

Cutie Pie

Ice Breaker

Ice Prince

Ice Giant

Cold as Ice

Ice Storm

Full-Length Titles

Crash into You

Fight for You (coming soon)

Kill for You (coming soon)

The Second Generation

A Blushing Bride for Christmas

Love Bites

Come Undone

Dripping Pearls

Echoes of Forever

His Christmas Miracle

Taken by the Hitman

Wicked Saint

The Ruined Trilogy

Physical Science

Wrecked

Wanton

Wicked

Ruined: The Complete Series

Illicit Love Series

Irresistible

Irrevocable

Irreplaceable

Irredeemable

Destination Romance

Romancing the Cowboy

Beach House Beauty

Standalone Titles

A Touch of Summer

Black Velvet

His Secret Obsession

Dirty Boy

Naughty Little Elf

Tempted by December

Devil's Deceit

A Bride for the Beast (writing with Fern Fraser)

A Hero for Her

Pretty Little Mess

Dear Mr. Dad Bod

<u>Easy on Me</u>

Easy Ride

Easy Surrender

<u>One Night with You</u>

Falling Hard

Model Behavior

Learning Curve

Angel Kisses

<u>Silver Spoon MC</u>

The Surgeon

The Heir

The Lawyer

The Prodigy

The Bodyguard

Silver Spoon MC Collection: Nichole's Crew

Silver Spoon Falls

Xavier's Kitten

Callum's Hope

Snow's Prince

Aurora's Knight

Silver Spoon Falcons

Leia's Playmaker

Aspen's Defense (coming soon)

Gabbi's Goalie (coming soon)

writing with Loni Ree as Loni Nichole

Dillon's Heart

Razor's Flame

Ryker's Reward

Zane's Rebel

Oral Arguments

Grizz's Passion

Garrett's Obsession

About Nichole Rose

Nichole Rose writes filthy romance for curvy readers. Her books feature headstrong, sassy women and the alpha males who consume them. From grumpy detectives to country boys with attitude to instalove and over-the-top declarations, nothing is off-limits.

Nichole is sure to have a steamy, sweet story just right for everyone. She fully believes the world is ugly enough without trying to fit falling in love into a one-size-fits-all box.

When not writing, Nichole enjoys fine wine, cute shoes, and everything supernatural. She is happily married to the love of her life and is a proud mama to the world's most ridiculous fur-babies. She and her husband live in Arkansas.

You can learn more about Nichole and her books at authornicholerose.com.

facebook.com/AuthorNicholeRose/

instagram.com/AuthorNicholeRose

twitter.com/AuthNicholeRose

bookbub.com/authors/nichole-rose

tiktok.com/@authornicholerose